Splashed in
Red

TIFFANY RYAN HAYES

PAGE PUBLISHING, INC.
New York, NY

First originally published by Page Publishing, Inc. 2018

ISBN 978-1-64350-926-6 (Paperback)
ISBN 978-1-64350-927-3 (Digital)

Printed in the United States of America

Dedication

To my dear mother, Robin. You have raised me up with unending devoted support. Thank you for being my rock throughout my life and for encouraging me to explore my creative side. I love you, Mom, with all my heart.

Chapter 1

A Halloween Party

The essence of beauty. Only those few words could so aptly describe the scene. An observer could look upon this particular area and feel that one had entered the gates of paradise. Country lands, green and lush, were nestled comfortably amidst the beautiful organized grounds throughout the wineries of Temecula Valley. In its midst, a mansion sat regally in its own right, surrounded by acres of landscaped greenery, although it was not an uncommon sight to come across richly built mansions around this particular area of Temecula, for each one was designed and constructed under the direction of the owner's unique and expensive style. Still, this particular mansion was indeed magnificent to behold. The hills around the estate were either lined with grape vineyards and fruit trees or blanketed in green grasslands with the occasional pop of color from the local wildflowers. The place was relatively serene, free of any disturbance. Although this area was near the city, it was still out of the way enough to consider it as "a country-like dwelling." However, despite its quiet surroundings, inside of the mansion walls was a woman who was in an absolute state of fret. Although she could be perceived to possess a calm and sensible nature, this time of the year seemed to snatch any semblance of that type of characteristic. The woman couldn't help herself, wondering out loud as she paced around wringing her hands in a nervous gesture.

"I really don't know what I'm going to do about the food. Every single recipe that I've looked at, so far, in those do-it-yourself magazines has had absolutely nothing to offer but some hellishly unappetizing food and drink involving a 'blood and gore' type theme. I mean, look at this page here. It's a prop skeleton laid out on a table, and there's a meat and cheese spread to indicate the organs in the skeleton's body. So disgusting! I mean, I understand that Halloween is a time for ghoulishly frightful ideas that are meant to scare even the hardest of horror enthusiasts, but if I were one of the guests being served something that looked like 'eyeball stew,' I should quickly lose my appetite." She paused her movement momentarily in order to concentrate. Her first finger curled and rested under her nose.

"Hmm, I wonder how I can prepare this feast without it being too Lily Munster-ish. Is that a word? *Lily Munster-ish?* What I mean is, horrifying under the guise of being hospitable."

Calista Serowik smiled to herself as she watched her mother pace fretfully back and forth from one end of the room to the other, swinging her arms this way and that as she moved. Margaret Serowik was especially known throughout the entire Temecula Valley as the "queen of Halloween" since every year, her house was the source of absolutely fabulous Halloween parties. The Serowik family house was more appropriately described as a mansion on an enormous estate nestled among one of the rich neighborhoods of Wine Country California. Margaret, a native of Binghamton, New York, moved to the West Coast after she met and married the heir of the prestigious Serowik Hospital.

Richard Serowik was a fun, charming young man who fell head over heels for the dark-haired, blue-eyed beauty, who was eight years his junior. After they were married, Margaret and Richard had lived a comfortable life of traveling, getting involved with various community activities, and raising their most valued treasures—a boy, Connor, and a girl, Calista. The children had been accustomed to a cushioned upbringing of privilege and prestige; however, their parents also motivated them to appreciate the luxuries they were both born into and to embrace ambitious attitudes when it came to education and a career.

Connor, the elder of the two siblings, had a late start where education and/or work was concerned, since his main ambitions after high school fell upon the achievement of a reputation of being a complete partyer and playboy. Even before he graduated from Everest High School, Connor had practiced his fence-jumping skills and had missed many days of school. Because of this, Margaret had to go down to the school and plead with Connor's teachers, who agreed to pass him after he completed a stack of makeup work and did not miss another day of school. At graduation, Richard gave his wife a diamond tennis bracelet as a reminder that it was her efforts that got their son his diploma. But Connor still had his wild streak even after high school, and was known about town as a hell-raiser. After a few DUIs and even a BUI, boating under the influence, Richard and Margaret took him under their care and constant watch until the boy could prove himself mature enough to return to the world as a civilized human being. When that would be, they had no idea. Richard was looking forward to that day; however, Margaret had all the patience in the world when it came to her son.

Just as Connor had taken upon the role as the bad boy in the family, Calista had chosen the role of being the good girl. She did not seem to have a single rebellious bone in her body. One could always find Calista at home or at the library, studying or doing her homework. She loved school and had embraced the message her parents had pressed upon her about doing something meaningful with her life. After high school, she immediately enrolled in college; and after four years, she soon obtained her license as a registered nurse. She worked at her family's hospital in the emergency unit and still lived at home with her parents and brother.

Calista was sitting comfortably on a sofa with a soft fleece throw blanket covering her outstretched legs. She was half listening to her mother's fretful rants and half deciding upon which outfits she liked best and which one she wouldn't be caught dead in, as she leafed through the pages of a clothing catalog. Nothing seemed to weigh on her mother more than her noted title as the Queen of Halloween."

"Mom," she said with amusement in her voice. "You're being ridiculous. I don't know what magazine you picked up, but there are plenty of available recipes around here somewhere that are appealing to everyone, especially people with squeamish stomachs. There are chocolate cakes with cookie or candy headstones. There are marshmallow ghosts and skeletons made out of pretzels. We can also serve punch for the witch's brew. It doesn't have to be gross, and we can still keep up with the whole authentic Halloween theme. We can even have just the regular festive holiday foods like turkey, mashed potatoes, pumpkin pie and cranberry sauce." Talking about food was making her hungry. Her stomach made little gurgling noises.

"Yes, I know, but I don't seem to be looking in the right magazines. All of these home magazines seem to feature food made up to look like severed body parts covered in blood or other bodily fluids," Margaret said. Then she added, "Look at this—bloody fingers, eyeballs in a pool of green punch, and look at this, a severed head with brains spilling out as a dip! Ugh, it makes me sick just reading these gory recipes! That is not going to go over well with the old-fashioned murder mystery party that I have planned. Everything needs to look nice and neat and civilized. I mean, after all, we are having a good old-fashioned civilized murder, not some disgusting reenactment of a horror film. Ew! Ew! Ew!"

"Don't worry, Mom. We'll have enough cute festive food, and the party will end up a success like it does every year. You worry too much. Besides, you have Connie to help." Connie was the family cook and an absolute genius in the kitchen. Whether the dish was sweet or savory, Connie's food could only be described with one word—excellent.

"I suppose you're right. It really is a spectacular event, and everyone invited talks so highly of it afterwards." She thought silently for a moment before adding, "Besides, if there is any of my guests not having a good time, I always make certain to keep the drinks plentiful and flowing. Alcohol has a way of bringing out an uplifting spirit in everyone."

Calista said, "Isn't the party planner you hired going to plan the food anyway?"

Margaret nodded. "Yes, she's a new choice for this year's party, which made me hesitate at first, but Joyce Galway is supposed to be the best in the business. She used to work in Los Angeles for some posh event-planning company, and now she has her own business out here in the wineries. Did you know that it only took a few months for her to make a name for herself out here? She is supposed to be literally that good. Anyway, Joyce specializes in weddings, both small and large, christenings, first communions, bar mitzvahs, and all sorts of various events. She also has connections with some higher-ups in Los Angeles and is somehow able to get celebrities to make appearances at events. It wasn't until I saw Gretchen Freemont, you know, the lady with the horses who lives in that gray house with the red brick roof just there down the road? Well, I was on one of my power walks when I saw her on my route. She was taking one of her horses out for some exercise, and we talked for a bit. Anyway, she mentioned that Joyce had just finished a training course in learning how to put together a successful murder mystery evening. So imagine my delight when she agreed to accept my venue. Oh, I know she'll benefit highly from our business. She does cost a pretty penny, but can you imagine how many other people will want her business for their own Halloween parties? They all probably begged her to plan their events. Makes me feel very special. However, I'm sure that she enjoys having me as a client since I compensate her well, and I like to contribute my own time in the planning and organizing, which ought to make her job a lot less stressful."

"Trust me, I've seen you in action. So much so that I wonder if all the party planners we've had over the years think that you're too much help. You have your own ideas as to how the party should go, and the party planner has a different idea in mind. Sometimes, Mom, you simply need to place a little faith in them. Besides, Joyce should have assistants to help her." She sighed.

"Ah, well. I'm certain it'll be a success this year as it has been in years past," Calista said. "And, as you mentioned before, Mother, you're paying her a pretty penny to do all the conducting. Why not just sit back and let her conduct?"

"Oh, Cali Girl," her mother said with a smile on her face. "What's the fun in paying for everything and not being able to put your own fingerprint on it? I want everyone to be able to recognize my efforts, and I like to show some pride for those efforts without feeling like some rich hypocrite who pays for everything, doesn't lift a finger, then takes credit for all the hard work."

Calista knew all too well how much better one felt when one worked hard instead of paying for rendered efforts. She was like her mother in that sense. Unlike her big brother, Calista had worked her way through nursing school before she graduated with her BSN. Her parents did give her a small allowance during college to help Calista have somewhat of a social life, but Calista had preferred to spend the money solely on a supply of food and drink, a small portable refrigerator, and a four-cup coffee maker. Her only real splurge was on fictional books, which she found to be comforting entertainment. During the weekends, when her fellow college mates were out going to the theater, having fun at bars, clubs, fraternity parties, and romantic dates, Calista preferred to stay in her room at the campus dorms and study. Being a homebody, she was never one to really party, and she didn't want a boyfriend to spend her free time with. Her brother had inherited all of the genetic partying traits for both of them.

Calista loved her brother and even envied his free spirit at times, but she could never be comfortable in his preferred environment. This helped her parents out a great deal since they didn't have to worry about where she was during weekend nights and could focus solely on where her brother was. They knew perfectly well that their responsible daughter was fast asleep in bed, and if she was awake, it was because Calista was at her little desk in her dorm room, studying until she couldn't keep her eyes open any longer. It all paid off in the end. Calista had graduated and got a job at her namesake's hospital. Calista had chosen to work in the emergency room unit of the hospital because she felt that it was a great experience for any nurse. Besides, she figured that her character was perfect for that area of the hospital, and that she could be an example of calming strength in such a crazy environment.

Calista was even happier when her college roommate, Erin Carney, had agreed to join her and to apply for the same unit. Erin lived in Temecula as well, in an average-sized suburban four-room house with her parents. The two girls took the least favorable shifts, which were mostly graveyard, and they remained close ever since. Erin had quickly become a favorite among the members of Calista's family, and Calista was glad that she had her best friend to offer companionship and support, especially during those stressful times at work when it seemed like everyone in Temecula was injured.

From her place on the sofa, Calista called out, "Hey, Mom?" She asked, trying to sound nonchalant as she leafed through the pages of her catalog, "What is the murder mystery going to be about?"

"You know better than to ask me that, Cali Girl," her mother replied. "This may be my first time doing this, but I know better than to reveal anything. The murder mystery has got to be a hush-hush situation before the party. But I can tell you that it's going to involve quite a few actors, some playing fellow guests, some murdered, and some acting as servants. There'll be a butler, we'll have a valet team, and, of course, the murderer. It should be a lot of fun figuring out 'whodunit.'" Margaret squealed in delight.

"And it's a dress up in any costume we want?" Calista asked. "That'll be fun."

"Yes, but I would prefer you to dress in something appropriate for the evening, meaning that I don't want anyone dressing up as some kind of modern character. I would like everyone to look vintage like the old horror films in black and white—Dracula, Frankenstein, and the Mummy. Then there's the old detectives like Sherlock Holmes and Poirot," her mother answered. "I want this to be as realistically old-fashioned as possible."

"Better put that in the invitations," Calista said.

"Oh, I did. In fact, I had Joyce design the cards and send them out herself. They all have that vintage elegant look. She does such a great job with that sort of thing. It will be the same amount of people invited as the years before along with one guest of their choosing, and they will have to share a room with that said guest."

The Serowik home was perfect for any large party with twenty furnished rooms; two pools with adjoining hot tubs, one indoor and one outdoors, and three tennis courts. People who were invited to the parties at the Serowik home were also expected to stay in one of the rooms until the next morning and leave only after being served breakfast. This was to prevent anyone from leaving the premises after an evening of gaiety and the consumption of alcohol. The mansion was almost like a hotel, conveniently located right there on the premises for the guests' comfort without them having to pay for it.

Margaret was still thinking about the party. "I don't want Connie to have to do all the cooking herself. It'll be a lot. I'll call Joyce today and ask her to recommend a good chef who can whip up some creative holiday dishes so that our party doesn't end up a disaster!"

Calista laughed, got up from her seat, and walked out of the room. Her mother could have a bit too much energy like a little toddler jumping around on the family's furniture, enjoying her own little quirks while ignoring anyone who looked on. In a way, she couldn't wait to have children simply for the fact that her mother would have some pint-sized playmates to keep her amused in that big mansion.

Chapter 2

A Stabbing Takes Place

The well-known dinging of the bell, followed immediately by the 911-dispatch orders came into one of Temecula's fire stations late Friday evening, forcing Medic Engineer Fitz Palmeri and his fellow colleagues out of their warm twin beds to the scene of an attack. It was a little difficult to understand at first since the dispatch was saying that they were expected to be at a stabbing, but it was unclear if there was just one person or more in need of medical attention. The fire crew stepped into their turnouts and hopped inside their polished red engine. Lights and sirens were turned on, the fire crew placed their protective headphones on, buckled up, and the engine took off toward the scene.

The call originally came from a bouncer at Scootin' Boots, a country western dance hall located in the oldest part of town, where the youth engaged in line dancing, drinking, and mechanical bull riding. It was a fun place to be except for the alleged stabbing that had reportedly occurred. When the engine rolled up to the scene, the ambulance was already parked outside the entrance. Fitz jumped from the driver's seat and grabbed his gear. There seemed to be just one person hurt—female, by the looks of it—and the emergency personnel were hovered over her desperately trying to treat what definitely looked like stab wounds covering her torso. There was so much blood, and the woman coughed out gurgling sounds. She tried desperately to breathe, but it was getting more difficult with each inhalation. After they did all they could for the moment, the team placed the woman on a gurney, slid her in the back of the ambulance, and rode with her to the hospital, still continuing their attempts to save her life, which seemed to be slipping away. It was clear to Fitz that the woman had a breast augmentation done before and that something sharp had torn into the right one because he could see and feel the viscous fluid of silicone mixed with blood oozing over her skin. Although he was busy concentrating on the woman's vitals, Fitz glanced up long enough to see that the woman was attractive and that the dress they had cut off her was one of those sexy tight-fitting dresses that women squeezed themselves into when they wanted to go out clubbing. The woman's designer boots were placed inside the ambulance before the back doors to the emergency vehicle were slammed shut.

The woman was unconscious at first but seemed to be coming to, coughing and spitting out blood from her mouth. She was in a pretty bad state. Fitz rested his palm gently on her forehead and told her to calm down, that everything was going to be all right. The woman screamed in pain and writhed against the straps holding her tight on the gurney. A female paramedic sitting across Fitz grabbed a vial of morphine and injected the woman with it. She then followed that injection with a promethazine chaser. Morphine often causes nausea, and the promethazine was to prevent vomiting from happening. Her muscles softened, and the writhing movements ceased as she slipped quietly back into unconsciousness.

Back at the hospital, one of the nurses was on the phone with a paramedic, getting the details of the incoming patient's current status. In spurts, she barked out the information as well as orders for any available staff to be at the ready for the incoming victim. This case was sounding dire, and fast response was crucial. Calista and Erin had joined a team of medical professionals ready to welcome the incoming ambulance carrying the female patient in critical condition. Someone was able to get a hold of the woman's identification card from her evening bag, which had been found lying in a pool of blood next to her body. The person who found it handed it gingerly to a gloved paramedic. The woman was twenty-five years old, her address was local, there was an indication that she was an organ donor, and there did not seem to be any previous medical conditions or allergies of any kind that would complicate her treatment.

The entire emergency room was filled with the type of chaotic control that only nurses and doctors were accustomed to. The gurney was pulled out of the vehicle in a swift and delicate manner. Each medical professional started working on the young woman as soon as they could get their hands on her. With the force of everyone's legs running, the woman was immediately wheeled into the operating room where Dr. Neville Williams, the available surgeon at that time, had been preparing to operate as soon as she was brought in. He had scrubbed and disinfected himself as quickly as possible before walking quickly into the operating room, and the doors closed behind him.

Calista could feel a bit of exhaustion caused by the aftereffects of the excitement creep into her bones as she watched the gurney disappear through the swinging doors of the operating room. She always felt that way whenever there was a critical patient. There was this motivational rush of excitement felt by everyone in the ER, and they behaved like robots. Their only thoughts were focused on their job at that moment, nothing more. Once the worst was over, and the patient was taken elsewhere, the same rush that had exploded now had the same exhausting effect on medical personnel. *This must be what druggies feel when they go on a high then a low,* Calista thought musingly. She looked down at her uniform and grimaced. It was splattered in blood. She turned to proceed toward the woman's locker room and collided into another bloody uniform, a dark blue uniform—the uniform of a fireman. His hands were quick and instinctive as he reached out and gripped her arms so as to steady both his and her balance. Calista looked down her arms and at his hands. She figured that it was a good thing that he had already taken off his protective gloves, which were most likely covered in bodily fluids as well. She looked up toward the fireman's face. A pair of light-blue eyes attached to a kind face stared down at her brown ones. Both Calista and the young fireman seemed to be tongue-tied for the moment. It wasn't an awkward moment. It was a-well-just-that moment. They just stood and stared.

Finally, the fireman spoke. His voice was deep and kind. It had a strong and soothing effect that reminded Calista of spa music.

"I am so sorry, Miss. I, um, didn't want you to fall." He continued to hold on tight to Calista's shoulders.

"Hi," Calista replied dreamily. She felt immediate euphoria staring up into his face. He was cute, really cute. With a sudden feeling of ridiculousness, she shook herself out of this state of mind and smiled up at him.

"I'm Calista, one of the ER nurses," she said. "I was just on my way to get cleaned up. Would you like to come? I mean, I could take you to where there's some place for you to wash your hands if you like."

"Thanks, but I have to get back to the ambulance. They're, uh, going to take me to my station, and I'll get cleaned up there. It's nice to meet you, Calista."

He gave her one last look before Fitz bounded down the hallway. He was gone so fast that Calista did not have time to wake from her reverie and ask him what his name was. When he was completely out of sight, she made her way to the locker room with a feeling of lighthearted happiness. There were not many men whom she found attractive, and it made her happy that she encountered one tonight. She wondered if she'd ever get a chance to see him again. Erin was already there in front of her own locker, and she was almost dressed in her extra pair of clean scrubs. Her bloody ones were gathered in a plastic bag on the floor, next to her locker.

"I am not looking forward to cleaning those. I almost think I should throw those away," said Erin. "They are awfully stained with blood."

"Just pour some hydrogen peroxide in the bag and let the clothes soak inside before you put them in the wash. That's what I do whenever my uniforms get crazy messy."

"That's because you wear scrubs that are mostly white with little animals printed in pastel colors. Mine is darker, and the hydrogen peroxide will make bleach spots appear on them."

Calista went over to the water basin and started to lather her hands and arms with soap. Erin, sitting on the wooden bench looked up toward her friend and motioned at her own face. Calista took the hint and checked herself out in the mirror to clean the blood spatter on her face in the area that Erin had pointed out. Once she had completely scrubbed every inch of her body and had put on a fresh uniform, both nurses returned to their workstations. Erin inquired as to where Calista was after the patient was wheeled into the operating room, but Calista just shrugged off Erin's question, hoping that her friend wouldn't catch on to the newly acquired shade of red on her cheeks. She wanted to get back to work but found it difficult to concentrate during the rest of her shift.

Erin was also full of energetic chatter about the excitement that just occurred. Both she and Calista were curious as to what happened that caused a young beautiful female to be brutally stabbed outside a popular local country western line-dancing club. However, despite her curiosity of the heinous event, Calista found herself glancing toward the back entrance of the emergency unit where the emergency personnel had wheeled in the young stabbing victim. She wondered if she would ever see that fireman again or at least get lucky enough to find out his name.

Calista finally shrugged her shoulders and sighed to herself, "Oh well. He probably wasn't interested anyway. He was really handsome though." She picked up one of her patient's paperwork and went to go check his vitals. *Back to work,* she thought.

About ten minutes went by when Calista heard her friend utter her name.

"Cali," Erin called to her friend. "Do those belong to that stabbing victim?"

Calista looked over to where her friend had pointed. Lying on the floor against the wall was a pair of designer cowboy boots, definitely feminine and definitely not the kind of boots that a woman would wear during a long hard day at the ranch. The tan leather was highly polished, and it had a swirled design over the front of the boot in bright colors of turquoise, red, green, and yellow. The boots were beautiful indeed and very stylish. Calista thought that they were pretty enough to wear to a wedding.

"It would seem so, but I'm not positive," said Calista. "If they are hers, I guess they might have gotten dumped after she was wheeled in." Calista went over to where they were standing, and she tentatively picked up the boots with gloved hands. She figured that the woman would want to have these back. She knew she would if they were hers. Curious, she turned the boots over to see if they were in her size. It wasn't like she was going to try them on, she told herself, but she was curious anyway. As she glanced at the bottom of the boots, a sound like crumpled paper hitting the floor caught her attention. Calista looked toward where the sound was. Just as she thought, a folded piece of paper had fallen from the inside the heel of the boot and onto the pristinely glossed hospital floor. Instinctively, Calista picked it up and, after a quick inspection, unfolded it and read the handwritten message, "Meet me outside the front entrance of Scootin' Boots, 10:00 PM sharp!—DUB."

"That's odd," said Calista softly. She looked at the time on her watch: 10:45 p.m. Clearly, this was a note written by the woman's attacker, and she should give this piece of evidence to the police. *Oh dear*, she thought suddenly, excited by this realization. Calista wondered who the woman that got stabbed was. She had heard the woman's physical stats by the emergency team but did not know her name. Plus, she was so taken by the fireman whom she bumped into that she didn't really care about the woman's identity at the time. *Ha! The power of eye candy*, she thought. *Good-looking men could be so distracting.*

Calista fetched a large plastic bag that was usually used to store patients' belongings. She placed the pair of boots in the bag after she replaced the piece of paper inside one of them. Once she made sure that they were completely sealed, Calista placed the bag in the only place where she figured it would be safe—her locker.

Chapter 3

Lieutenant Ram Nandyala and Sergeant Bartholomew Lee stood over the area where the body of a stabbed woman once lay. After the ambulance had taken the poor woman away, the two police detectives had now stared down at a mess of blood. Crime scene professionals were busy taking samples and collecting anything that would be construed as evidence in bags to take to the police department's laboratories. Lights from cameras shot out around the crime scene to preserve anything that looked important. Even though the woman was not there anymore, the scene had still remained grisly.

Lieutenant Nandyala instructed Sergeant Lee to take notes while he interrogated various witnesses. Since it was a Friday night, there were plenty of people to question. Dozens of handsome men who looked like they exited a modeling photo shoot, dressed in jeans and designer shirts with their hair perfectly styled, were questioned. As far as females were concerned, it looked like the entire group of Miss America candidates was present. Women who appeared to be ready for some serious partying looked like they were almost too hot to handle, and they knew it. Long shapely legs and plunging necklines seemed to be the dress code at this place. Some wore cowboy boots dazzled up to give a sexy cowgirl look. All women wore smiles on their perfectly made up faces. The women were used to men ogling them; however, in this capacity with the detectives approaching them in such an official manner, it seemed to cause a bit of excited alarm among them. Each one couldn't wait to talk to the detectives, and all seemed to want to monopolize the detectives' time talking about themselves rather than the tragedy itself.

However, both detectives were used to dealing with such an attractive glare that they hardly ever squinted nowadays. Lieutenant

Ram Nandyala was an older gentleman, and although he had treated each witness with careful ease, he did have a certain method of dealing with persons of certain femininity, especially those who were oozing it at him, by steering the conversation back to the point of the matter. The lieutenant questioned the men with a mutual respect of male understanding. Although he had been successful with women over the years as a detective, it was so much easier to question men. They held nothing of a distracting exterior, and so it was easier to concentrate on the subject at hand. Women, especially those who looked as nice as these ladies appeared, did hold certain distracting qualities. Women, in Ram's experience, were so unpredictable that one did not know exactly how to approach them, no matter how prepared one was.

He also understood that women held this unearthly power over men, and that they had the ability to manipulate any situation toward their own agenda. Ram had learned to question women differently by transforming his demeanor into a persona of humility. He treated women with a tone of reverence and higher regard than he had for himself. Men were mostly good at retelling details of concrete observances. Women, on the other hand, could do much more than that. He did not view men and women as equals in society. Instead, he regarded women with a sense of awe and honor. Women to Ram were above men and would always remain so throughout time, so he had to take tentative measures when dealing with women. *The female mind,* the lieutenant thought, *is a very valuable witness because it seems to possess an innate sense of particular vibes, whether the vibes are positive or negative.* Women may not know where these intuitive feelings originated, but they feel them just the same, and the detective knew that it was women who held the most important information as bystanders.

Sergeant Bartholomew Lee enjoyed watching his lieutenant during interrogations. Lieutenant Ram Nandyala had once explained to Bartholomew of his ideas regarding particular differences that dwelled within the average man and the average woman. Whether or not Bartholomew Lee had agreed with his lieutenant's reasoning, he thought that the whole idea was definitely interesting. There were a lot of interesting things about Lieutenant Ram Nandyala. Although he was an exceptional police officer and had embraced the strict standards of his title and rank in the homicide unit, Ram Nandyala was also a man who was not afraid to reveal his true self and to indulge in the things of life that pleased him. Ram was often seen in his office practicing yoga and lighting incense as a means to meditate upon a particularly challenging case. Ram did not disclose too much about his personal life, but Bartholomew knew that the lieutenant was single, a born bachelor, and that he would most likely stay that way. He was the type of man who did embrace romance, but more as an onlooker rather than an active participant. Ram was married to his career, and he had this unique way of merging his personal amusements with his job so much so that he seemed to be quite content with his life as it was with no desire to alter it. Some officers had whispered about Lieutenant Ram Nandyala as being quirky, a bit odd at times, but everyone agreed that the man was an efficient, reliable, and a well-liked individual. Ram was friendly, open-minded, accepting, and had made it a point to treat any person he came in contact with, even criminals, with the utmost dignity. It was that positive character about him that many an officer wished he or she could emulate.

Sergeant Bartholomew Lee was well aware of his boss's unconventional mannerisms, theories regarding human nature, and his ideas about unsaid commonalities of each gender. He also knew that the lieutenant had never steered him in the wrong direction during their previous cases together. Therefore, Sergeant Lee had never questioned nor argued with Lieutenant Nandyala. Instead, he just sat back within himself and absorbed all he could of the lieutenant's methods.

Although Lieutenant Ram Nandyala was born in California, his parents raised him to embrace both the American customs as well as their own native Indian culture. Ram was an intelligent man, genius in fact, and he had built up the reputation of solving almost every case he was given. However, the secret to his success was not his intelligence, although that was a major contributing factor. Ram had approached each of his cases with methodical care and precision.

He was not one to dive into cases with gusto like a kid jumping into a pool not knowing the temperature. He approached a case from the outside, formed a plan of how he would approach it, and slowly worked his way inside, peeling back the layers of information until he came to the nucleus of the case itself. Then he would make his way out again, reviewing details, and compartmentalizing them. He made it a point to review every detail at every angle, whether important or not, no matter how long it took. It was important for him to be thorough.

He never treated suspects as if they were suspected at all, even and most especially if he felt absolutely sure of their guilt. His demeanor allowed most people to feel at ease in his company whether they were in possession of a guilty conscience or not. He had such a humane way of dealing with suspicious individuals that some culprits would admit their guilt even though Ram had not begun the process of grilling. Whenever a case was solved, fellow officers would let out ejaculations of triumphant cheers. But Ram would not partake in such celebrating. Instead, he would be seen walking toward his office, closing the door behind him, and carefully gathering all the evidence together to be stored away.

He had explained to Bartholomew one time that the reason for this little ritual was because he was not as eager to solve a murder mystery as he was obtaining justice for a victim and to bring some semblance of peace to the victim's family. When he packed up the remaining effects of a murder case, he would use that time to think about the victim. Ram would even talk to the victim in his head and have that moment of collaborative closure. It was an unusual way of doing things, but it was his way, and he was not ashamed of admitting it. Sergeant Lee considered himself lucky to be Lieutenant Ram Nandyala's partner. He trusted the lieutenant's every move and never questioned a single request from him. The two men worked very well together and, in the end, usually "got their man," so to speak.

At their current crime scene, they learned from the various club patrons that the stabbing victim's name was Joyce Galway, a local event planner whose work contained nothing but glowing reviews from her clients. She was also a woman who enjoyed the nightlife of the city. People seemed to know her pretty well as a fellow partyer. From what they could ascertain from the woman's bloodstained body, Joyce was a beautiful young woman, and she was dressed in an outfit that was ready for an evening of entertainment. It was easy to see that the woman was most likely a favorite among the men and possibly a subject of envy among the women, although the other women at the club seemed to be able to hold their own.

Although Scootin' Boots was a regular hangout of hers, it was not the only place she frequented. Sergeant Lee was able to jot down a few other names of bars and clubs that Joyce Galway liked to attend. There was a Crystal Chimes, Hidden Hookah Hangout, The Mist, and the various wineries that made up most of Temecula's charm. The two detectives planned to visit these other places as soon as possible. They tried to get through all of the patrons at Scootin' Boots as quickly and as thoroughly as possible since they did have to visit Fire Station 27 and Serowik Hospital to talk to other possible witnesses: paramedics, doctors, and nurses who had direct contact with the stabbed woman. Once they were finished gathering as much information as they could for the time being, the detectives got in their car and drove to the fire station to question the paramedics who were first on the scene and had tended to the victim.

Chapter 4

At station house 27, there was a major buzz regarding the evening's terrible events. Each of the firefighters had their own idea as to what must have happened. It was quite the source of gruesome gossip. Although they were used to blood and gore during their careers as firemen, they hadn't begun to imagine experiencing something like this before. Before the shift began, the only calls they could have expected that night were heart attacks, overdoses, and traffic collisions caused by drunk driving. The traffic collisions were where most of the blood and gore came from.

A couple of police detectives were present at the station when Fitz arrived in the ambulance. The detectives approached him as he walked up to the garage where the fire engines were parked. One was a tall thin man with lean muscles in all the right places, middle-aged, and of Indian descent, with a full head of thick black hair perfectly combed in a conservative style. The man had greeted him with a very kind smile on his face. The other man, a bit shorter than the first, was as white as the first man was tanned. He had brown hair, looked to be around thirty years old, and he had a serious look on his face as if he was constantly thinking of something very important.

"Mr. Fitz Palmeri?" the first man asked. Fitz nodded. "Yeah, that's me, sir."

"Hello, I am Lieutenant Ram Nandyala," said the detective who was clearly the superior of the two. "And this is my colleague, Sergeant Bartholomew Lee."

"Bart, please," insisted the second detective. Fitz shook hands with the two police detectives and asked to be excused to take a quick shower. Both detectives agreed. By the time Fitz returned, the two detectives were comfortably seated at the station's dining table.

Sergeant Lee was busy writing in his notebook while Lieutenant Nandyala was happily sipping a cup of tea. Obviously, the lieutenant familiarized himself with the kitchen and boiled himself some water for his hot beverage. It amused Fitz to see the lieutenant sit there looking like he was in his own home instead of a fire station. Lieutenant Nandyala acted so calm and serene as though he hadn't a care in the world. The lieutenant was unlike any police officer Fitz had seen before in his life. The man was clearly of Indian descent even though his accent was American. His manner was so mild and reassuring that Fitz could not help but feel at ease in the man's presence.

Ram Nandyala noticed Fitz standing there mentally scrutinizing him and his partner, and still wearing his smile, beckoned the young fireman to sit. He offered a cup of tea to Fitz, which Fitz first declined. The lieutenant insisted, explaining that the brew was from his family recipe and one in which he kept on his person at all times for occasions such as this.

He proceeded to explain to Fitz as the young fireman took a tentative sip then another more eager gulp. "My mother used to prepare this brew for me as a child to drink before studying for my tests in school. She was a very wise woman who believed that a calm mind was an open one and ready to absorb knowledge easily. It contains a hint of ginger to calm the stomach, which is necessary during unsettling events such as this. Nowadays, I use the same blend to serve to witnesses whenever the opportunity presents itself. It helps to relieve one's stress so that one may remember things that he or she would either forget or consider too irrelevant to even bring up."

Fitz nodded his understanding.

Ram said, "I know that you are used to treating patients on calls who are, shall we say, in a pretty messy physical situation. That is why you make a good witness. You can separate yourself from the emotional part of the scene and simply focus on the reality of it. It sounds cold, I know, but that is what makes people in your position efficient at their job."

Again, Fitz nodded and added a, "Thanks, man."

"Good," continued the detective. "Now, if you please, relax your body, close your eyes, and concentrate on the detailed events of this evening. When you arrived at the scene of the attack and first approached the woman lying on the ground, did anything strike you as odd, other than the stabbing itself?"

Fitz, his eyes closed and his mind in a complete state of relaxation, tried to paint in his mind a reenacting picture of the scene that had happened only a short time previously that evening.

"The woman was lying on the pavement," Fitz said. "Blood was splashed all over her upper body and oozing out, creating pools at an alarming rate. There were people dressed up to go clubbing, standing around in horrified awe, craning their necks, wanting to see the victim's red-stained body but not wanting to get too close so as to save themselves from stepping in the mess. It wasn't too difficult to get to the woman's body. I could tell that her blood pressure had plummeted because her pulse was up, and her skin was cool and clammy to the touch. It took a couple of us to quickly find her wounds and put pressure on them. Believe me, we couldn't work fast enough. There were so many of them." He remembered the gaping wounds, thrust in so angrily and deep. "Whoever stabbed her was full of rage for that woman."

He couldn't remember anything suspicious, and he didn't know how the attack happened. The only thing he had concentrated on from the moment he had gotten the call was to save the patient's life, nothing else. Fitz relayed these thoughts to the detective, who looked at his partner. Sergeant Lee finished scribbling in his notebook then nodded at Lieutenant Nandyala. Lieutenant Nandyala smiled at Fitz, thanked him for the information, handed Fitz his business card in case Fitz should think of anything else later on, and the two detectives proceeded to leave. Fitz watched them go then turned to his cup of tea. Although he couldn't quite pinpoint the herbs used to make it, Fitz found it delicious. It was the kind of tea that needed no sugar or lemon. He drained the red-colored liquid until the final drop had trickled its way down his throat.

The detective was right, he thought. *My mind does feel open, and my body feels calm and yet, at the same time, rejuvenated. It's kind of weird, but I like it.*

Fitz looked down at Lieutenant Nandyala's business card. He wondered if the detective would mind if he called to ask for the tea's ingredients. It seemed like a strange thing to do, but there was something about that detective that made Fitz realize that the lieutenant was definitely a unique individual in the police department.

The two detectives had just slipped back into their unmarked police vehicle when the call came in. It was 11:30 p.m., and the message was not good. The woman who was stabbed outside Scootin' Boots just an hour and a half before was pronounced dead in the operating room, despite all the efforts of the surgeon to save her. The detectives looked crestfallen as Sergeant Bartholomew Lee put his keys in the ignition and started the car.

"Well?" asked Bartholomew. "Where to now, Lieutenant?"

"To the hospital," replied Ram. "We'll need to talk to the staff and find out if they learned anything that may prove useful."

Chapter 5

Calista had just finished her clinical reports when two well-dressed gentlemen holding shiny badges, indicating that they were the police, surprised her. The older of the two spoke. He was a tall man of Indian descent, handsome with a full head of glossy black hair, sprinkled with a little gray, and perfectly combed. His voice reminded her of an energetic cup of espresso and cream, smooth and appealing when consumed. Calista had never met anyone like him before, so authoritative and yet at the same time not intimidating. He reminded Calista of her grandfather so much that she imagined him to be the type of man whose knees children would want to sit on so that he could tell them a fascinating story—a story that would include a wise moral at the end.

"Hello," the man said. "I am Lieutenant Ram Nandyala, and this is Sergeant Bartholomew Lee." The man next to him, holding a notebook and pen, offered a quick friendly wave.

"We would like to speak to the medical personnel here at the hospital who tended the woman who was stabbed this evening."

"Oh! That was me." Calista sounded excited then stopped. "What I mean is, I was one of the nurses who was present during her arrival. My name is Calista, by the way. Calista Serowik."

Ram said, "Serowik? Is the hospital related to your namesake?"

"Yeah, it's my dad's family's hospital," Calista said in a matter-of-fact tone. "It's the main reason why I wanted to become a nurse. Kind of like working for the family business."

"Excellent, your father must be very proud of you," the lieutenant said in a smooth tone of voice. "We would like to ask you a few questions and then if you will please direct us to those who also came in close contact with the victim."

"Sure," said Calista. "What do you want to know? Oh wait! You're the police, so you might want to see this before anything else occurs. Follow me please."

The two men exchanged amused glances while they followed the young pretty nurse to a door that read, "Girls Locker Room." The two men instinctively hesitated, and when Calista noticed this, she continued to beckon them in.

"It's okay," she whispered. "The place is usually empty around this time."

"Still," Sergeant Lee said and looked pleadingly at his boss. Ram took the hint. He turned to Calista.

"Still," he said, smiling. "Why don't you do a thorough sweep so as to not shock any potentially present females."

Calista agreed and made sure that the locker room was empty. The two men waited patiently until they saw her head peek out the door to face them.

"Coast is clear," she said cheerily.

The three of them walked through rows of lockers until they came to a locker that read, "Calista Serowik, RN." Calista reached into the pocket of her nurse's uniform and retrieved a key, which she used to open the padlock. Once the door was open, the two men peered in to see a large plastic bag. Calista held it toward them, and Sergeant Lee took it and placed it on the bench so as to examine its contents. Ram used gloved fingers to rummage through the bag and retrieve the boots inside. Calista then led their attention to the piece of paper inside the boot.

As Lieutenant Nandyala held the paper, Sergeant Lee glanced over and read the words written on it.

"'Meet me outside the front entrance of Scootin' Boots, 10:00 PM sharp!—DUB.'" Ram's eyebrows were raised and furrowed.

"That's cryptic," he said. "I wonder what it means. You say that you found this inside the boot just like it is now?"

Calista nodded. "Well, I stuck the note back in the right boot, but I can't remember if it came out of the right or left boot. When I turned the boots over, the note popped out and hit the floor before I saw it. It's weird," she said. "The woman seemed to know and trust the person who wrote this note, and since she was dressed to the nines, the author of this note seemed to know that Scootin' Boots was a regular hangout for her."

Sergeant Lee said, "So maybe DUB was a friend. But why would a friend simply use his initials? Ah, because he was planning to stab her. But why use initials at all. Why write a note that could be traced back to him at all, when he could have arranged a meeting with her in person?"

"Who says Ms. DUB is a man?" said Calista. "A woman could easily stab another woman. It doesn't take a lot of strength, and since the victim wasn't expecting an attack, she would not expect to defend herself."

Ram said, "I agree. What other thoughts do you have about the victim, Calista?"

"Heck, if I know," said Calista. "I don't even know who the victim was, just that she died."

Sergeant Lee consulted his notes before answering, "A Ms. Joyce Galway."

Calista yelled, "SHUT UP!"

The two men jumped. Calista's outburst surprised them.

"You know her?" asked Ram.

"Well, no, but—yes, I do. Holy cow. Mom is going to have a hernia." Calista's hand went to her head. She looked entirely distressed.

"And why is that?" asked Ram.

"Because Joyce Galway is the event coordinator of my mom's annual Halloween party, and this year, it was going to be really special since my mom was planning a new theme—a murder mystery theme. I didn't know Joyce personally, but I had met her at my parents' home when they were doing the planning. Oh crap! I wouldn't want to be in Mom's shoes right now."

"Nor in Ms. Galway's shoes," said Ram pointedly.

Calista snapped out of her misplaced grief. "Oh yes, I'm sorry. How selfish of me. That poor woman to be stabbed in such a monstrous manner." Calista silently wondered how horrible it would be to wake up one day, only to have one's life tragically taken. And how tragic it would be for Calista to break the news to her mother. It was still the thirtieth of September, and early enough for her mother to get someone else to coordinate the party, but the murder mystery would most likely be canceled.

"So," asked Calista, "you have any leads as to who may have done this?"

"None so far," said the lieutenant. "Do you have any insight or more evidence to contribute besides these boots, and the note, of course?" Ram smiled as he held up the pair of boots while Sergeant Lee held open the bag. "This is a big help, by the way." The men secured the boots back in the bag.

Calista said, "No, just that. I only had the boots because they were left by the ambulance entrance doors, and figuring they belonged to the victim, I stored them for the police." Ram gave her an impressed look.

"Do you know who operated on Ms. Galway after she was wheeled in?" asked Ram.

Calista replied, "I think so. If he's not in the surgery room, he should be in his office filling out his report on the stabbing. Usually with incidences as tragic as tonight's, it is better to jot down the details quickly while they're still fresh in one's mind."

"And where would I find his office?" Ram asked.

Calista directed the two detectives out into the hall and down a series of turns until she approached an office door with a brass-plated marker that read, "Dr. Neville Williams." She knocked and turned the knob. A deep male voice inside beckoned the incoming visitors.

Calista said, "Hey there, Neville, these gentlemen are detectives and want to talk to you about the stabbing that occurred earlier this evening." The detectives introduced themselves to Dr. Williams using their full rank and title.

The doctor, who was seated comfortably in a brown leather swivel chair at a large mahogany-stained desk, was in the middle of writing on a form. *That's probably the report the nurse was talking about,* thought Ram. The doctor stood, gave Ram and Sergeant Lee a warm smile, and gestured for them to have a seat. Ram accepted the chair while Sergeant Lee remained standing, a notebook in his left palm, a pen interlaced in his right fingers, and ready to take notes on the conversation. Calista had already left, closing the office door softly behind her.

The doctor was a young man, about thirty years old. He had dark curly hair, blue eyes, and a pleasant-looking disposition.

Ram folded his hands, placed them in his lap, closed his eyes for just a few moments then, opening them, spoke with his normal coffee-and-cream-like tone of voice.

"First, Dr. Williams, may I express sympathy during this obviously stressful evening. It must be very difficult to lose a patient, even one with whom you do not personally know. I need to ask you a few—"

"Actually, Lieutenant," Dr. Williams began, stopping Ram in mid-sentence, "I did know the victim."

"Really?" Ram's eyebrows lifted.

"I mean that I didn't know her well, but I did cross paths with her from time to time. We went to the same water holes, you might say." When he noted the confusion on the two detectives' faces, he explained, "The same bars and dance clubs."

Ram nodded his head, and the doctor continued.

"So yeah, I didn't know her too personally. The closest we got was on the dance floor." His smile was now a sheepish grin. Ram thought, *It seems that the good surgeon has skills inside and outside the operating room.*

"It must have been difficult operating on her wounds," added Sergeant Lee, concern in his voice.

Dr. Williams thought about that before answering. He said, "It does seem that way to most people, but for a surgeon, we are trained to block out any personal emotions during surgery. The reason for this conditioning is to prepare us for situations such as operating on our own mothers to operating on a sworn enemy of ours. In any such case, our job is singular—to save the life of the person before us on the table."

Ram smiled and said, "A very noble cause. However, when you did cross paths with her, even if they were of an indirect nature, how would you describe her? Would you say that Joyce Galway was a woman who possessed a kind nature?"

Dr. Williams grunted. Ram waited for his response. A shade of red appeared on the doctor's cheeks, and Ram ascertained that his reaction was unintentional. The doctor looked down at his paperwork as he tried to explain.

"She didn't seem like the type who would be nice or kind or anything of that category."

"Can you explain?" asked Ram.

The doctor now shifted uncomfortably in his seat. He was clearly not enjoying this interrogation. "Well, there was this one time when I was at Crystal Chimes, and I could see that she was there as well. Joyce was served a drink from the waitress, and after taking a sip, she threw the drink straight into the waitress's face. Then as cool as a cucumber, she firmly placed the glass back onto the waitress's tray, said something to the fact that her drink was not what she ordered, and sent the waitress back to the bar, wet and shocked, to correct the drink order. Then she went up to the hostess, hollered for a manager, and once the manager arrived, she demanded that her drinks be absolutely free due to the incompetent type of service she was issued, and the manager, trapped in a corner by her outspoken anger, gave in to her demands." Dr. Williams looked at Ram. "Let's just say that she got good and hammered that evening, and that in itself is not a pretty sight. It was pretty embarrassing for everyone who watched her antics that night. However, it's not the first time she's made a scene out in public."

"How so?" asked Ram curiously.

"She was belligerent when she had a few too many drinks in her system. From the condition of her liver, I had to open quite a bit of her torso due to the many stab wounds, I could see that she enjoyed her liquor a bit too much. And I do know that she was a, well, a …"

"A?" coaxed Ram.

Now the doctor's face was beet red. "She was"—he cleared his throat—"well, she liked to sleep with many men." As soon as he said that, Dr. Williams tried hard to avoid the lieutenant's face.

"I see," said Ram. "And by any chance, would one of those men be you, Doctor?"

The man sitting across from Ram was now transformed from this confident surgeon who saves lives down to a pathetic child who just got caught with his hand in the cookie jar.

"From the look you're giving me now, it would be easy for me to decipher that you did know her at a more personal level. A more— shall we say—intimate level?" The doctor, still looking down, just nodded his confirmation.

Ram's tone was both authoritative and kind. "Dr. Williams, I am not here to chastise you for having anything to do with the victim, and I do understand that this is a delicate issue for you to talk about openly with us." Ram looked up behind him where Sergeant Lee stood. "But I must insist that if there is anything to reveal, we are the people to reveal all you know. It will not only help us with the investigation, but I can assure you that your secrets are kept as confidently safe as possible as long as it proves to be irrelevant. You do not have to be worried about us leaking any of the information outside this room unless it is absolutely relevant to finding out who stabbed Ms. Galway. I have a feeling that Nurse Calista would not appreciate learning of your relationship, though brief, with Joyce." The lieutenant and the doctor held gazes of understanding across the desk. Dr. Williams took a deep breath and let it out.

He said, "It was just a one-time thing. I was drunk, she had had a few, and we were both in an amorous mood. We walked to a hotel located just a few blocks down, rented a room for the rest of the evening, and she was gone before I woke up late the next morning. It was just the one time, and I never called her after that. In fact, I didn't even get her number. I did see her from time to time at the local nightspots, but she didn't seem to remember me, or she did remember but just didn't care. Joyce always had a new man she was fawning over, or she was busy laughing it up with a group of girlfriends. In fact, I don't even think she remembered our evening together. It's scary when you think about it. I could have been a rapist or a murderer, and she would have simply walked into a trap ready and willing." Dr. Williams suddenly remembered that the woman was murdered and that the killer could have been anyone in that club. He shared this last thought with Lieutenant Nandyala.

Ram nodded and confirmed that they were still unsure as to who they're looking for. They asked a few more questions, thanked the doctor for his time, handed him their cards, and made their way to the hospital exit, the bag of boots and note held firmly in Sergeant Lee's hand.

When they got in the car, Sergeant Lee could not help but comment, "So our good doctor has got some groove in his move." Then he added, "Pretty trippy to be operating on the same woman with whom you had a fling."

Ram nodded. "Not just that, a woman who conveniently forgot that said fling." He thought for a moment. "Dr. Williams didn't strike me as the type to slough off such an experience. He seems like a bit of a romantic."

"Not the type to 'hit it and quit it,' huh?" asked Sergeant Lee. Ram looked over at him with an amused expression.

"No, Bartholomew, not that type. I think we'll call it an evening after we bring the bag back to the forensic laboratory. Tomorrow, we'll pay a visit to the medical examiner and get her opinion of the exact cause of death and anything else she can offer."

"Sounds good," said Bartholomew, and the two men drove off to the police station in silence.

Chapter 6

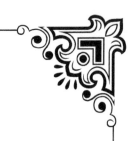

It was late Monday morning when Fitz Palmeri was finally able to leave work. After that horrifying call that led him and his colleagues to a horrific stabbing, the transport to the hospital, talking to the police detectives, and the few other emergency calls that pulled him from his bed, Fitz was completely exhausted. When his relief showed up promptly at eight, Fitz decided to lie down for a nap before he drove home. He didn't want to get into an accident due to sleep deprivation. While he rested, his mind wandered to the thought of his meeting with the pretty nurse, her dark hair, creamy skin, and pretty chestnut-colored eyes. *Stupid, Fitz,* he thought. His attraction to her had rendered him so tongue-tied he forgot to tell her his name. Before he drove home, he might find the courage to stop by the hospital and ask her on a date. *No, that wouldn't be good,* he thought. He checked his watch. *By now, she would be finished with her shift and wouldn't be there.*

"However," Fitz said to himself, "if I simply leave my number with a fellow employee to give to her, maybe it will save me the embarrassment of a possible rejection."

Although Fitz considered himself a pretty good-looking young man, his short stature had caused a bit of a break in his confidence. He wasn't picky when it came to a girl's height as long as she was attractive, but apparently, it was a deal breaker for many girls who were taller than him. Calista wasn't taller than him. In fact, she was quite petite—tiny, to be precise—so why was he so nervous thinking about asking her out? Girls, Fitz realized, were so much more powerful than boys. The strength of ten muscular men could not compete with the power of a delicate girl such as the beautiful Nurse Calista.

By the time he arrived at the emergency room, Fitz felt he had already eliminated a quart of perspiration caused by nerves and a sudden onset of a knotted stomach. He searched the middle console of his truck for his stash of paper napkins that he had accumulated during his many trips through fast-food drive-ins, grabbed a handful, and wiped the moisture off his forehead. He walked into the unit to find it only somewhat busy. He figured that since he was still wearing his uniform, no one would question his entering through the back entrance where only ambulance transports were allowed clearance.

He went to the nurse's station and asked a nurse, who looked like the only thing she was busy with was a cell phone conversation, which he guessed was with her boyfriend. He waited patiently while the nurse giggled and twirled a strand of her golden hair. When she spotted him, the nurse's demeanor suddenly changed to annoyance. She whispered a quick goodbye to the person on the other end of the line, pressed the end button on her phone, and glared pointedly over at Fitz.

"Hi," said Fitz, trying to sound nonchalant. "Is Calista working at the moment?"

The golden-haired nurse's glare soured. "How did you get in here?" she asked coldly.

Fitz pointed toward the sliding doors. "There," he said.

"You're not on duty?" She appraised his uniform. Fitz shook his head.

"Then not only am I not going to answer your question, I'm going to have to demand that you leave." She pointed toward the same doors. Fitz didn't move.

"Now," she said with more insistence.

Fitz smiled back at the scowling face and said, "Oh, I could leave now—or I could inform the human resource department here at the hospital that this is the tenth time I have caught you on the phone with your boyfriend instead of tending to patients who need their vitals checked and medication administered."

It only took a moment for the scowl to melt into a look of frightened surrender. Fitz knew that he had hit home and continued. He grabbed a pad of paper and a pen, saw that the pad was a stack of prescriptions that belonged to Dr. Neville Williams, ignored the fact that it was not a stack of blank notepaper, and wrote his name and phone number on the top sheet.

"Now if you could deliver a message to Nurse Calista for me, I can promise that your frequent personal cell conversations will go ignored." Fitz then peeled the sheet off, handed it to the nurse, and headed back to where he came in, but not without noting the look of reluctant defeat emanating from the golden-haired nurse's face.

When Calista Serowik clocked into work to begin her Monday evening shift, one of the nurses on the opposite shift, Nurse Caroline Reese, surprised her with a folded piece of paper. Calista thanked her and, curious, unfolded the paper to find that it was a sheet from one of Neville's prescription pads. She read the name *Fitz Palmeri* scrolled on it along with a phone number. Wondering whose name this was, she looked up and opened her mouth to inquire, only to see that Caroline had walked off and had completely disappeared from view.

Staring down at the name and number, she tried to figure out who this Fitz was. Fitz sounded like a cool name, like it belonged to a fun-loving guy. Maybe even a cute guy. Of course, it might be possible that this was a mistake, and Caroline handed the paper to the wrong girl. Then she stopped her thoughts. Could the name Fitz belong to that handsome fireman who wheeled in the stabbing victim, Joyce Galway, the other night? She certainly hoped so, but Calista also realized that could be reaching. The fireman that night, her mystery man, didn't seem at all interested. To the contrary, he seemed annoyed by her friendliness.

Calista decided to ignore the name and number for now. She folded the sheet in half and slipped it into the pocket of her smock. She then smoothed back her hair and stood up straight before she returned to work.

Chapter 7

Hans and Ingaborg Krause

Rita's Roses was a popular floral shop located near the wineries, especially since the owners catered to most of the winery's everyday floral decor. The owners, Hans and Ingaborg Krause, were standing in the middle of their shop facing the two detectives, Lieutenant Ram Nandyala and Sergeant Bartholomew Lee, and trying to answer the questions handed to them to the best of their abilities. Lieutenant Nandyala had been tipped off by one of the patrons from Scootin' Boots that Joyce Galway had engaged the business of Rita's Roses to provide all the plant arrangements for most or all of her planned events. However, Joyce had severed all business ties with that particular floral shop, and the detectives were curious as to the reason behind the severance.

Ram watched the couple in front of him. The man was long, lean, and muscular. His demeanor was welcoming. Hans, Ram could ascertain, was a good-looking man with a full head of thick honey-colored hair and a closely shaved beard to match. Ram did not think that the beard suited the man.

The woman, however, was no more of a match to him than a tulip to a bird of paradise. It wasn't that she was ugly or even plain to look at, but the scowl Ingaborg held so firmly on her face seemed to destroy any semblance of beauty. She was tall as well, thin with a sharp definitive facial structure that seemed to dare anyone to argue with her decisions. If Ram could describe Ingaborg Krause with just one word, it would be this—*frightening*.

Although the woman was clearly intimidating Sergeant Lee, who inadvertently stood a foot behind Lieutenant Nandyala, the latter was undeterred by this woman's inadvertent attempt to scare. Nonetheless, Ram wanted to make this interview as quick and painless for everyone before leaving. After the necessary introductions from both parties, Ram immediately dove into the reason for his visit.

"I have been told by one of the witnesses at the crime scene, where Joyce Galway was murdered, that she had at one time been in a business relationship with the two of you and had recently severed that relationship due to an unfortunate occurrence. Would you care to shed light on that for us please?"

He waited patiently for their reply. Behind his right shoulder, Sergeant Lee was ready with his pen and notebook.

It was at this moment when Hans, appearing at first kind and confident, quickly changed to sheepishly guilty. His cheeks, once the color of cream, were now transformed into two large maraschino cherries. He looked down at the floor and kicked at something that wasn't there.

His wife, on the other hand, now held a look of triumph. Her face still had that permanent scowl, but now it looked to be more like a sneer. She gave her husband an icy glare before answering the detectives.

"It was I who had to extinguish the business relationship between Ms. Galway and our floral shop. She was proving to be an absolutely horrible client, always overworking us to provide more than our services could offer. Her demanding jobs were beginning to interfere with any amount of free time, what little there was, that we had. *Especially* my husband's." She looked pointedly over at her husband, whose cheeks now resembled a couple of bright-red apples. His face remained planted on the floor.

"Of course," Ingaborg added with venom in her tone, "Joyce was always like that growing up—always wanting men to not only pine after her but to also do special favors at her request. Girls as well were constantly trying too hard to get into her good graces. Joyce was like one of those popular girls whom everyone wanted to be noticed by. Why, I don't know. It wasn't like she was anything to look at."

"You grew up with Joyce Galway?" asked Ram.

"Yes, and once upon a time, I thought that she was my friend. But thank goodness that only lasted until about second grade. I was one of the lucky students who saw through her shallow fake-friendliness and thus kept my distance. By the time middle and high school came around, I was already wise to her manner of manipulation."

"But why did you agree to do business with her?" Sergeant Lee asked. He was starting to feel a little less wary around Ingaborg.

She sighed, "By the time we were older and had established a good starting point in our lives, I thought that it would be okay to do business with her, especially since she was doing very well out here. And why not? We were both adults who were trying to grow our businesses! But I was wrong, so stupidly wrong. Joyce was still the same hypocritical little bitch that I remembered as a child. So I cut all ties with her, and we have not seen her since."

Ram looked at Hans for confirmation. He nodded his head to confirm Ingaborg's statement. Sergeant Lee opened his mouth to ask another question, but Ram gave him a look that made him stop. Ram turned to the couple and said, "Thank you for your time. Here is my card. Please call if you think of anything that may be important for me to know."

Ingaborg took it upon herself to escort the detectives toward the shop's front door. After she shut the door, Ingaborg turned to her husband, who was trying desperately to avoid her by concentrating on a tulip arrangement.

"Happy now?" Ingaborg hissed. Her mouth was now full of heated words, and her voice was ready to hurl them at him all at once in a great ball of fury when the door behind her reopened, and Lieutenant Nandyala's head appeared.

"So sorry to bother you again," he said profoundly. "But I noticed that you have an herbal garden growing on the side of your store."

Hans perked his head up from behind a pot of tulips. "Yes, those are my little project," he said. His wife, now fuming from the interruption, simply rolled her eyes.

Lieutenant Nandyala did not seem to notice. "I was wondering if I could ask you a few questions as to how you manage to grow some of them in this particular type of climate." Ram said to Ingaborg, "I hope you don't mind, madam, if I steal your husband for just a few minutes of his knowledge. I'm sure it will benefit my own method of gardening." Ingaborg, still scowling, walked out of the room in a huff. Hans followed the detective outside.

As they stood over Hans's garden, Ram noticed that the man's demeanor had returned to a relaxed happy state. It was evident that Ram's interruption had saved Hans from an emotional beating.

Hans asked, "So, Detective, what is it that you want to know?"

"What I want to know has absolutely nothing to do with your garden," Ram explained. "Getting you out here without your wife was a bit of a ruse, even though this garden is an impressive creation of yours." Ram spread his arm over the herbs as an indication of this comment.

"Then how did you know it was the garden that would bring me out here instead of Ingaborg?" Hans asked. Then he remembered the little wooden sign nailed on the side of the garden box that read, "Hans' Herbal Garden." He smiled and nodded. "Go ahead, Detective, ask away."

"How long were you having an affair with Joyce Galway?" When he saw the man about to protest, Ram held up his palm. The tone in his voice was firm, "Don't ask how I know, Hans. I'm not here to revel in your dirty laundry, nor am I here to accuse you of murder. I am here to establish an understanding of the real Joyce Galway. I believe that you can help, but we don't have enough time to discuss extensive details since your wife doesn't seem like the type to let you alone to converse with others without her present. Simply answer my questions, and I'll be on my way." When Hans nodded, Ram continued.

"How long?" he repeated.

"Seven months," Hans reluctantly answered.

"Does your wife know?"

Hans nodded.

"Is that the reason why she stopped your business relationship?"

Another nod.

"Have you been in contact with Joyce since then?"

"No."

"Has your wife been in contact with her?"

A pause, then Hans said, "No, I don't believe so."

"Were you the only man Joyce was involved with?"

"No, she was the type to 'hit it and quit it.'" When Ram's eyebrows rose, Hans said, "She didn't believe in getting a boyfriend, only into collecting one-night stands. With me, I guess it was different because I was some type of forbidden fruit, being married and all. Joyce liked to obtain that which wasn't hers, and she seemed to enjoy watching relationships break up because of her. It gave her some feeling of power. I know that she's angry right now, but Ingaborg's a good woman, a strong woman, and I behaved badly toward her. I'm not saying it was Joyce's fault, but she is such a beautiful woman who knows exactly how to turn a man's head and hold it there until she's finished with him, not the other way around, and I was just one of the weak idiots who fell for her charm."

"Can you name anyone else who was involved with her?" Ram asked.

Hans shook his head, "Ingaborg's and my time is already consumed by the business that we aren't aware of anything nor anybody that doesn't involve our shop. I don't even know how I managed to have an affair, especially for that long." Hans looked up at a window located on the second floor of their floral shop.

"Now that Ingaborg knows everything, our little circle is even tighter. She won't let me out of her sight." Hans had a defeated look on his face as he explained this to the detective. As if on cue, Ingaborg's head appeared at the window, looking down, her face framed by the lace curtains. The scowl on her face could sour cold milk in a minute.

Ram thanked Hans for speaking frankly with him, and soon the detectives left. Hans watched the police vehicle retreating down the road before returning to the front door of his business and the ever-marital clutches of his spiteful wife.

As Ram and Bartholomew drove off together, sharing their thoughts about the visit with the Krauses, a call came in over the radio for their immediate attention. Another stabbing had occurred, this time at a local hangout not far from where they were at that exact moment. Ram and Bartholomew took one look of astonishment at each other before Sergeant Bartholomew Lee slammed his foot on the gas pedal toward the scene while Ram navigated the route.

Chapter 8

A Second Tragedy

By the time the fire engine arrived behind the ambulance, Fitz, along with the rest of the crew, had been informed by dispatch that the stabbing victim was a twenty-five-year-old female, no known medical conditions or allergies to medications, and currently sustaining multiple stab wounds to her torso. The stabbing had occurred at Crystal Chimes, a popular hangout for the sociable youth as well as those young at heart. The victim's blood-soaked body was found inside a small hallway that led to the bathrooms, and the woman who found her body had made even more of a mess by trying to apply CPR. The woman screamed for help, and soon a waiter came by to see what the commotion was. The woman who found the victim, a middle-aged individual, was quick and efficient with the situation at hand. She instructed the waiter from where she knelt to grab the woman's purse, which was lying on the floor, and to get out her identification and dial 911. When she saw that the young waiter was stiff from the shock, she yelled at him for not moving quick enough. The waiter, a young twenty-year-old, finally snapped out of his obvious shock and obeyed the woman's orders. Because the waiter had the victim's driver's license in his palm when he called, the dispatch operator was able to reveal the identity of the victim: Clara Morton.

When the medical response team finally reached their patient, Fitz could see that the young woman was suffering tremendously. She had labored breathing, and she was expelling massive amounts of blood from her body. He also noticed that this woman was also an attractive female just like Joyce Galway, and that the stab wounds held a striking resemblance to the wounds that were inflicted on Joyce. He wondered for a fleeting moment if there might be some sort of connection between the two crimes. Instinctively, he shoved that thought to the back of his mind as he went through the repeated motions that he had undergone just a few days ago.

Again, Fitz rode to the hospital, and once again, he helped to wheel in the second stabbing victim to the operating room of the emergency unit. And, once again, he had encountered the attractive nurse named Calista whom he had been secretly hoping to run into again, just not under the same morbid circumstances.

Calista, who was also in her mode of serious medical duty when the call came in to prepare the emergency unit of the severity of the patient's condition, could not help herself feel a little leap of joy in possibly seeing that cute fireman once again.

After the young woman was sent through the swinging doors that led to the operating room, Fitz, while stripping off his protective disposable gloves, made a 180-degree turn to the nurse's station to seek out the nurse named Calista. She wasn't there, but it didn't take long for him to wait. Calista appeared from around a nearby corner, and when they spotted each other, both Fitz and Calista walked toward each other. When they were just a foot apart, facing each other, neither seemed to know what to say. Then Calista spoke.

"So, Mr. Fireman, you didn't have to stab another victim as an excuse to see me."

"Huh?" Fitz was taken aback by her comment.

Calista said, "I'm sorry, that was in poor taste. We have a very morbid sense of humor here, and sometimes I can take it too far."

Fitz smiled. "No, I get it. We get the same way at the station. Seeing the humor inside the tragedy helps one to separate oneself from feeling too much emotion. It's a coping mechanism that helps people like us to do our jobs better as professionals. But maybe this time, your joke was a bit too soon."

"Do you know who she is?" asked Calista.

"Yes, dispatch told us. It's, um, wait a minute. Hang on a second, I know it. Clare—no! It's Clara something. Yeah, now I remember. Her name's Clara Morton."

He paused, and they stood in silence.

Calista, feeling suddenly embarrassed, said, "Well, sorry to bother you then." She turned and walked away.

Fitz called after her, "Wait, Calista." She paused as he walked up to her. He touched her arm.

"I'm sorry," he said. "That was rude of me. Let's start over, shall we? I'm Fitz, Fitz Palmeri. I was a bit tongue-tied the other night, especially after the stabbing that I didn't get a chance to introduce myself. The stabbing shook me up more than I expected. I guess that's what happens when a person goes through something the first time. The second and third times, one can get more used to it. It's not that I want to go through it again and again. Anyway, I left you my number with one of the daytime nurses. Did she ever give it to you?"

Calista nodded. "Caroline, yes. She gave it to me." Calista reached inside her pocket. "I thought it might be from you, but couldn't be certain. Sometimes we nurses get numbers, and we have to be careful about calling them. We don't want to get in touch with a potential stalker, you know."

Fitz laughed. "I realized that after I left the message, but my mind was so tired from the night before. I should've added a description to my name, like 'the hot medic engineer you bumped into last night.'" Now they both laughed.

"I like your confidence. Well, I'd better get back to work, and it looks like you do too," Calista said and indicated toward three other uniformed firemen looking ready to go, waiting for Fitz with cheesy smiles plastered on their faces. Fitz and Calista both hurried toward them.

Before they approached the other firemen, Fitz whispered to her, "Um, do you want to catch some dinner sometime when we're not working?"

"Sure," Calista whispered back. "How about this, I'll call you since I have your number."

"Cool," said Fitz. He smiled at her. *Should I give her a hug good-bye or shake hands?* he thought. But Calista had already answered that for him. She quickly got behind her nurse's station and was already picking up a stack of orders as she waved at him and told Fitz to have a good night. He waved back then joined his coworkers.

Fitz felt pretty good about himself. He had a date with a really pretty nurse. Soon, he had hoped. He didn't want to feel too confident in his own male charm, but he felt certain that she'd call him soon. He tried to hide his excitement from the other men in the fire engine, but they had already detected his emotion and were all set to tease him as soon as they were out of earshot.

"So, Palmeri, who's the brunette?" his buddy, Tyler Riley, asked, nudging Fitz in his ribs.

"Yeah, dude, she got a sister?" asked another paramedic named Shawn Cowl.

"You mean, does she have a brother?" teased Nick Beringer to Shawn.

Shawn shot back, "Whatever, just don't ask if she has a mother, Beringer. Everyone knows you like them older, much older!"

Beringer feigned a look of hurt as he clutched his chest and replied, "You know very well it was late at that winery, I was drunk, she looked hot for a fifty something year old, and she paid for the taxi and the hotel room, which was a suite by the way."

"Yeah, and that rock she sported around on her wedding finger was a good indication that it was her husband who ended up paying for everything," said Cowl.

"Do I detect jealousy in your voice?" asked Beringer.

Shawn Cowl smirked. "Yes, I am so jealous I wasn't able to do some old woman with sagging crepe paper for skin."

As the two men—or boys, for that matter—spewed jabs at each other for the duration of the trip back to the station, Fitz breathed a sigh of relief that the focus of their attention was off him for now. He enjoyed his fellow coworkers, but sometimes he felt that he could clobber them.

Later that evening, after their visit to Crystal Chimes to study the crime scene and question various witnesses, Lieutenant Ram Nandyala and Sergeant Bartholomew Lee paid a visit to both Firehouse 27 and Serowik Hospital's emergency unit for a second time that week. They had to make a new set of inquiries after finding out who could be identified as a possible witness. It was during these inquiries that the news came. It seemed that whoever had stabbed and killed Joyce Galway just a few days before had now claimed another victim, for it was confirmed by the hospital that Ms. Clara Morton had succumbed to her injuries and was declared dead on the operating table.

Lieutenant Ram Nandyala sighed. He rubbed his eyes in an effort to wipe away the exhaustion he felt inside. This case was definitely going to be time-consuming, and if they didn't find the killer, the police would run the risk of having a third murder to solve.

Chapter 9

The Serowik mansion and entire estate was majestic and regal on the outside. Lush green bushes and lampposts were perfectly aligned along the red brick walkway up the navy blue front door. However, behind that closed navy door, it was a truly chaotic scene from a madhouse. Margaret Serowik was nothing but a blustering bundle of nerves and hyperventilation. When Calista came home from work in the morning and told her mother of the second victim stabbed the night before, the guttural scream emanating from her mother's lungs could shame a banshee.

"Mom, what the heck?" Calista couldn't understand her mother's outburst.

Margaret cried out, "Do you know who Clara Morton was? She was one of Joyce's friends who agreed to be an actor at the party! She was to be one of the maids at the murder mystery dinner! Now what am I going to do? My party planner has been murdered as well as one of the actors. Who's to be murdered next? My butler? In any case, I am already running behind with the plans, and now I have to hire someone else to coordinate the party. Do you think that it's possible to get another planner who can do a murder mystery? Oh, and I have to get someone to help cook and bake and, and—oh!" Margaret's hand went to her forehead as she let out a long groan.

"Mom, how can you be so insensitive?" Calista retorted. "These women lost their lives, brutally, for that matter, and all you can do is worry about your party? I didn't think that we were still going to have one after what happened to Joyce."

"Oh, Calista, my dear, give your mom a break."

Calista turned to see their cook, Connie, come into the room where Margaret and Calista were, holding a tray of tea and cookies.

"Hosting wonderful parties is the one thing that really motivates her, and it wasn't her fault that those poor girls were murdered." She lay the tray down on a nearby table before adding. "Although, when I think about the way those girls were killed, it chills me to the bone." Connie looked over to where Calista was sitting.

"You need to be careful, my dear," she said to Calista. "It's not a safe world for young women to be alone in public, especially at night. It wasn't like the old days when women could walk the streets at night without fear of getting raped or killed. Nowadays, people are so evil out there. Right now, evil has come to our town and settled in comfortably. There's a maniac out there, killing young women, and anyone could be his next victim, even you!" Connie shuddered at this thought.

Calista thought that this type of thinking was normal for people of older generations. Most people who were at least fifteen years older than her would say things like "Back in my day, things were so much better, streets were cleaner, and there were no bad people to be frightened of." Calista remembered people who were teenagers in the sixties, a time when drugs and free love were the accepted style, now had the gall to complain about today's youth and how corrupted and disrespectful teenagers were nowadays. It confused her because she understood the sixties as a time when the youth had zero respect for their elders, and yet here they were, a little older, complaining about the very people that they once were. In that case, the youth of every generation had the same disrespect for their elders, and their elders complained about the youth's rebellious nature. She wondered if she would adopt this same view about life in general as she got older, scoffing at those younger than her when, really, she was no different than them when she was their age.

But then again, she didn't have any issues with any generation, older or younger, and felt that she would grow into an old lady who was accepting of the future generations and the changes that would inevitably come with them.

"Aw, Connie, you're so sweet. Nonetheless, you don't have to worry. I'm not the partying type of girl. Now my brother, on the other hand—well, you know, he parties for the both of us." She smiled at this. Connor was quite a wild boy, one who, since he was born, kept his parents on their toes with constant worry, but she had to admit that along with his wild streak, her brother had this charm bred in him since birth that allowed him to shine at any gathering. Connor had the ability to simply walk into a room, and every female could sense the sparkle he held within. Parties did not seem to begin until Connor walked into the room. Girls swarmed around him like a bunch of fat kids fighting over the only cupcake. But even though they were formed from two completely opposite character molds, Connor and Calista were close siblings. They leaned on and appreciated each other's strengths and weaknesses. Out of all the females in the world, no woman knew her brother like Calista did. And no one held his ultimate respect and love. It didn't matter if he was getting attention from a group of lingerie models or on a date with an extremely attractive woman, all Calista had to do was say the word, and he'd drop whatever or whomever he was doing and rush to his sister's side. Calista, of course, made sure not to abuse this privilege.

Connie had to agree with Calista. "You're a good girl, Cali. I could never find myself foreseeing you as being one of those slutty girls who have absolutely no respect for themselves and who frequent those nightclubs wearing nothing but sparkling scarves that they call dresses. And they start out young. I mean, look at these young children dressing like little beauty pageant contestants. I blame these mothers, of course. Mothers just do not seem to care about their children's moral upbringing nowadays. I remember in my day, mothers took the time to care and to really stress good standards in their daughters." Connie shook her head in a disappointed manner and walked out of the room.

Calista began to pour her mother a cup of tea. "Here, Mom. This will help you to calm down a bit. You're acting like a nervous squirrel." Calista took a few cubes of sugar from a little silver dish and stirred them into her mother's drink.

Gratefully, Margaret took the cup offered to her and sipped. She inhaled the aroma, took a deep breath, and let out a long sigh. Tea definitely had the properties of being a cure-all for anything that negatively affected the human body or mind. In Margaret's mind, everything that had recently happened was too overwhelming and seemed to be ruining her plans for this month. The tea, of course, was soothing, and a cup of it along with a heaping scoopful of sugar made her feel much better.

Both Calista and her mother sat in silence as they drank their cups, and it wasn't until a few more moments passed by when Connie reappeared.

"There are two men to see you, ladies. One of them says that they're detectives and wish to ask you a few questions," said Connie. As if on cue, Detective Lieutenant Ram Nandyala entered behind Connie. He was dressed in his usual sharp suit, and the lieutenant had revealed a dazzling row of perfectly polished pearly whites. Behind him, Sergeant Bartholomew Lee followed with his usual pen and pad in hand. Ram walked in with a delicate catlike maneuver, took one of the available seats as if he was a family friend just visiting, and greeted the ladies with warmth. Bartholomew watched his boss as he adjusted himself so comfortably within the environment of the mansion. It seemed that any home they entered, Ram Nandyala had this ability to conform himself to the environment itself as if he was part of that environment. Even if the presence of the police was not a welcome entity of the residences, Lieutenant Ram Nandyala was never seemingly deterred by any hostile manner or behavior. In this case, however, the witnesses were not only kind, both Margaret and Calista seemed relieved to see the detectives there. Calista was calm and cordial, enjoying her tea as she sat chatting with the lieutenant. She offered both of the detectives a cup, which they both gratefully declined.

Margaret, on the other hand, was in no state of calm whatsoever. It seemed that one cup of tea was not enough. She jumped on Ram with a dozen questions, all of which she wanted answers to immediately. What was going on? Who was committing these murders? What is the police department doing about these murders? And so on.

Ram quietly and patiently listened to her as he sat, quite comfortable, one leg crossed over the other. He did not seem to be amusing Calista's mother. On the contrary, through all of Margaret's rants of anxiety, her arms flaying this way and that as she paced from one corner of the room to the next, Ram gave her his undivided attention, wearing a genuine look of concern. Calista was quite impressed with his method of dealing with her mother. *The man could calm a hungry lion,* she thought, because that was what her mother was emulating right now, a lion hungry for answers. Lieutenant Nandyala was a human-size walking, talking tranquilizing dart. Calista secretly wished she could be Sergeant Lee for just one day to watch the lieutenant perform his magic at work.

Ram said, "I know how terrible this is for you, Mrs. Serowik."

"Please, Lieutenant, call me Margaret." Calista's mother had recovered from her fretful state and was back to her role as hostess. "Can I get you something? Coffee? Tea? Soft drink? No? All right then." She appraised Ram's appearance and asked, "Where are you from, Lieutenant? India? You don't have an Indian accent, but you do look like you hail from that part of the world."

"Mom!" Calista said, horrified and embarrassed by her mother's crude frankness. Really, her mother could be too much to bear.

Margaret, realizing that her question may have been somewhat crass, immediately tried to make amends. "Oh, do forgive me, Lieutenant. Sometimes I have absolutely no filter when it comes to social matters. One would think that I have better manners when it comes to talking to foreigners. Oh dear, there I go again. You just look so exotic, which is actually a compliment, but how stupid of me. I mean that you aren't a foreigner because this is America, and all people of every shade of color are in fact Americans and are not foreign at all. What I should have asked is, where are your ancestors from?"

Ram smiled compassionately at her and replied, "California, born and raised. But yes, Margaret, you are correct. My parents emigrated here from India and have raised me up to embrace the American culture as well as also to understand and appreciate my Indian culture. Do not worry, my dear lady. You have not insulted me."

Margaret recovered from her embarrassment quickly. "I should hope not," she said. "You have a most beautiful shade of golden brown skin that many people would kill to have, Lieutenant."

"Thank you, and my name is Ram." Lieutenant Ram Nandyala then got down to the reason for his visit.

"From what we have learned, your event coordinator, Ms. Joyce Galway, was murdered. Ms. Galway was in charge of managing a murder mystery evening for you. After that, one of the girls who were hired to be one of the evening's actors, Ms. Clara Morton, was also murdered. Both women were friends from childhood. That much we know so far. What I'd like from you both is any information you can add or if you can point us in the direction toward possible witnesses who can also provide something useful that would help us to solve this case."

Now Margaret was excited. "So you came here to see if we might hold an important clue vital to the case?"

Ram nodded. Margaret let out a little squeal. What started out as a frightening tragedy was now turning into a game of mystery and clues, and she was finding herself enjoying the adventurous sense of it. Calista could see this and rolled her eyes. Her mother was such an unpredictable woman, dramatic and fun; but she could also be inappropriate in certain situations. If Ram had noticed this about Margaret, he did not give any indication. Instead, he continued to smile at Calista and her mother.

Calista said, "I don't think that we have much to add, Detective. Joyce Galway was an employee when it comes down to it, nothing more. And Clara Morton was the same. It seems to be a crazy coincidence that these women have been killed after my family hired them. We didn't really know either woman personally. Right, Mom?"

Margaret tossed her daughter and the detective an affirmative nod.

"In fact, neither Joyce nor Clara has anything to do with us," Calista continued. "Not in the personal sense, I mean. We never invited them, never hung out with them, nor were they friends of friends. They were hired to do a job and that was that. I don't think that their murders had anything to do with our party—oh, wait a minute!" Calista stopped herself to think.

"Yes?" Ram encouraged.

"Have you spoken with the husband and wife owners of that floral shop? What was it called, Mom?"

"Rita's Roses," her mother answered.

Calista said, "Yes! Joyce had collaborated with them to provide the floral arrangements for the party."

"Yes," said Margaret. "And I invited them to join us for the party as well."

"Yes, but don't you remember, Mom, that Joyce had a falling out with them recently and tried to get you to cancel your order. It was a bit dramatic."

Margaret nodded. "Yes, but of course I didn't. Whatever was between them was just that—something that they all had to figure out for themselves. I don't know why they cut all business with each other. Both Joyce and Rita's Roses provided excellent products and services, and together, they could have much success. If they no longer wished to work with each other, that's none of my business."

Calista added, "I think I know what the rumors were, although I'm not sure if there's any merit to them. You know how people like to talk about some juicy local gossip, and before you know it, the simple gossip has turned into an embellished scandal? Well, from what I heard, it seems that Joyce was getting too close to the husband at Rita's Roses. He's such a nice and friendly sort of person that some people perceive his friendliness to be flirting. Of course, it's probably because he's also so handsome. Some people have to be careful of such a notion. Misconstrued perceptions can cause awkward moments, don't you think? But even if it is true that he's such a flirt, one really doesn't know if he acts upon his flirtations. He could be just like a dog with all bark and no bite. However, that's just my perception. His name is Hans, and he's very good-looking, so of course the first reaction anyone makes regarding him involves sex. Not only that, he's a bit of a charmer, always courteous and complimentary to both men and women, mostly women, of course. One might say that he chose the right profession, owning a flower shop while possessing such a romantic disposition."

"And the wife?" Ram asked.

Calista frowned and thought. "Ingaborg is definitely a business woman, but she doesn't hold the charm of being a good saleswoman. I don't visit the flower shop very often, but when I do, it's only Hans whom I talk to. I have tried to include her in the conversation, but when I ask her something, she just answers with a word or two and doesn't continue to engage in the conversation. Oh, she's cordial to me, but it's he who keeps the dialogue flowing. In fact, personally, I think she is a bit of a cold fish, but I can't blame her. If I had a play-boy for a husband, I'd soon lose my self-esteem and trusting person-ality and that would harden anyone, man or woman."

"I agree with you. You do seem to have a keen perception of people's personalities. That is a good quality to possess. You'd make a good detective, Calista. Are you still having the murder mystery dinner?" Ram asked.

Calista looked at her mother. "Mom?" she asked.

Her mother sighed audibly. "I certainly hope so," she said. "I've had to contact the event coordinator that I've used in the years past, and he referred me to another company that can do the murder mys-tery theme."

"I see," said Ram. "So the present situation with the murders occurring hasn't frightened you into canceling this year's festivities?"

Calista made a noise that sounded like a guffaw. "Ha! A tor-nado could come through this town and destroy all the homes in Temecula, and Mother still wouldn't cancel the party."

"Oh, Cali Girl, don't be so rude!" Margaret said. "You're mak-ing me look very callous in front of Ram here. Of course, I would cancel the party if a disaster as big as a tornado swept through here, but there hasn't been a tragedy as big as that happening around here, so naturally, the party is still scheduled."

Calista said, "Of course the tragedy of two horrific murders is not that big of a deal." To this, Margaret stuck her tongue out at her daughter.

"Are Hans and Ingaborg still coming to the party?" asked Ram.

"I think so," said Margaret. "They haven't RSVP'd yet, but I'm sure this whole murder business has gotten them spooked for the moment. I feel confident that they'll call soon to say that yes, they'll come."

Calista lowered her chin and concentrated on drinking her tea. Margaret Serowik would never allow a little thing like a murder or two to spoil her plans for an event. *After all, the party must go on, mustn't it?* Calista felt a bit embarrassed. Her mother could act like such a rich snob at times, but the way she did it was simply so comical that no one could ever get angry at her because of it. Her mother was too much, and Calista loved her for it. With Margaret Serowik around, there was never a dull moment to be found.

"I must admit that I am concerned of the fact that you are still going on with this party. Two of your employees have been murdered. One of them had a falling out with two of your guests due to their own personal reasons. Even though it may be irrelevant, I do believe that it is important to be safe than sorry, and I am obligated to advise you to cancel this year's Halloween party."

Calista was nodding her head in agreement with the lieutenant. Margaret, on the other hand, was absolutely horrified. Her eyes grew wide and flared in anger as if they were daring Ram to repeat that last remark. Ram ignored this.

Margaret said, "I cannot believe that you would suggest such an abominable idea! Do you know how many years it's been since I have been hosting this Halloween event? Successfully, I might add! Nine years. Nine! And if you think that I am going to simply call it all off just because some idiot has been killing off some of the people connected with this party, well, Lieutenant Ram Nandyala, you are seriously mistaken!" Margaret couldn't help to straighten her back, hold her head high, and stick her nose up in the air as she said this. Bartholomew appeared intimidated by her angry outburst. However, Ram continued to listen with a calm demeanor.

He said, "Well, then, if you wish to be obstinate about this, we're going to have to come up with an alternative means to ensure some kind of a safety net for you, Margaret. I can arrange a few policemen to come to the party, posed as waiters or guests, to keep an eye out for anything that may seem suspicious."

"Why don't you come to the party?" Calista asked.

Margaret clapped her hands once and said excitedly, "Yes, Ram, why don't you and uh—" She gestured toward Sergeant Lee.

"Bartholomew," he answered her implied gesture.

"Why don't you and Bartholomew ..." Margaret started to continue then stopped and stared at Sergeant Lee.

"What a nice long name," she said.

Bartholomew didn't know whether to say "thank you" or "my apologies," so he remained silent. Margaret seemed to be in a better mood now that she was discussing her party. *My goodness,* Bartholomew thought. *The woman is like a light switch.* She could be angry one moment and happy the next. He wondered what it was like to live with a woman like Margaret Serowik. He concluded that Mr. Serowik must be a very brave and patient man.

Margaret continued, "That is such a good idea. Why didn't I think of it? Both Ram and Bartholomew can join us at the party as guests. After all, my guests are handpicked by me, and it will be our little secret that the two of you are actually real detectives." Margaret clapped her hands again and said gleefully, "Oh, this is too, too perfect. We are going to have the best Halloween party in Temecula!"

Ram said, "Very good. And now I have another question to ask you. Margaret, can you give me your impression of Clara Morton?"

Margaret stopped herself and scrunched up her face in concentration. "Well, I don't really know," she said. "I mean, I only met her through Joyce, and she seemed to be a nice person, very pretty too. She had these green eyes that were very striking. She only came over a couple of times to take a tour through the house with Joyce and to take notes on the rooms that would be used for entertainment. It's important that all the actors know their way around the house before they plan out the scenarios."

"What about you, Calista," Ram said turning to her. "Did you form an opinion of the woman?"

"Well," Calista began. "I met her one time here, and just like Mom told you, Clara was polite and nice. I did know her, well, *of* her, back during my days at school. She's a few years older than me. I had a good friend named Kerinsa Cadle, and Clara dated Kerinsa's older brother, Michael, in high school. We all went to Everest High. Kerinsa told me that Clara had broken her brother's heart after a few months of dating him and that he was affected pretty badly because of it. I guess he was head over heels in love with Clara. I felt sorry for Michael, but I didn't know him as well as I knew his sister. And I certainly didn't know Clara personally."

Ram smiled and stood. He shook hands with both Margaret and Calista, handed each of them his business card, told them to call at any time no matter what the hour, and the two detectives exited the room to leave.

Margaret finished her cup of tea and said excitedly to her daughter, "Well then, Cali Girl, since the party's definitely back on, let's get to work on making it a success!" Calista followed her mother out of the room, rolling her eyes up at the ceiling and shaking her head. Margaret Serowik was definitely an entertaining woman to know.

Chapter 10

Ram was jotting down some of the notes in chronological order that Bartholomew had dictated to him on the chalkboard in his office. So far, they had two murders, a few witnesses, a few potential suspects, but nothing really concrete since they still did not know what the motive was. They had a few theories though. The stabbings could be the act of a homicidal maniac. It could be that a jilted lover or a jealous girlfriend or wife had killed the women. Both men and women, feeble as well as strong, have the ability to wield a knife to kill, so that left a plethora of people to interrogate during the process of elimination. But one thing was a connecting fact that tied the two murders, and that was their connection to the Halloween party that Margaret Serowik was hosting. That was a good clue to pursue, but the only one they had so far. The killer left no fingerprints or incriminating DNA at either of the scenes.

Ram could not help but admit that this was the part in an investigation that was the most difficult. It was moments like these when he would regress deep into his mind and enter a state of concentration. He walked over to his electric tea maker and turned the heat on. He scooped a spoonful of dried herbs from a tin he always kept in his desk drawer into a strainer capsule. The herbal blend was a mixture from his home garden. Once the pot started to whistle its high-pitched tune, indicating that the water was at boiling point, he prepared a cup. He inhaled the rising steam from his cup and sighed with satisfaction. There was nothing like a homemade organic blend to draw out the essence of vitality within one's inner core. That and yoga were the two most important things that Ram believed were the secrets to his success. Oh, the years of intense training and developed maturity were definitely the reasons as to why he was considered the best of the best. Ram had learned how to read people like a psychologist. He had learned to detect if people were lying or telling the truth.

But tea and yoga represented a simplistic indulgence that allowed Ram to concentrate on his current case on a plane separate from the world of consciousness. It was during these moments when he entered a trancelike state that usually led him to either crack the case or at least break through an important detail that needed help.

An hour went by, and at the front desk of the police station, two men entered and asked to see Lieutenant Ram Nandyala. The front desk officer led them through to the homicide unit where Ram's office was. As the two men were announced, both Colin O'Darby and Kieran Ryan stopped in astonishment.

As the officer left them, the two men couldn't seem to move from under the doorframe. It wasn't because they were uncomfortable. It was more of astonishment that they felt as their eyes took in the scene before them. Inside the office was a plain-clothed officer, a bit stout and looking quite serious. It was Sergeant Bartholomew Lee standing next to a chalkboard, writing a few notes on the board. That part of the scene was normal enough. However, their eyes fell on a tall, tanned Indian man, also in plain clothes, positioned against the wall, standing on his head. Lieutenant Ram Nandyala's socked feet were directly pointed toward the ceiling. His entire body did not move.

Ram greeted the two astonished visitors, still in his upside-down position, and offered the two men a seat. As they tentatively walked in, they could see that his head was nestled comfortably atop a blue satin pillow on the ground. He studied the appearance of Colin and Kieran through his arms planted on either side of his head to help keep his balance.

As soon as their guests took their seats, Ram carefully positioned himself back into the upright position.

"You must pardon the initial perception of my appearance. I stand on my head so as to release any toxins from my body. It is very good for one's mind as well, although it does cause a bit of a spectacle." The two men looked over at Sergeant Lee, who pretended to notice nothing out of the ordinary. He simply stood facing them with pad and pen ready to take notes. Kieran had thought that Sergeant Lee would make a wonderful secretary.

"Thank you for coming in to see me," said Ram. "Was there anything that you would like to tell me before I ask you some questions?"

Colin cleared his throat and spoke first. "Well, sir, we were at Scootin' Boots when that girl was murdered. We came in because you had asked everyone who was there to contact you if we had any information, and, well ..." He looked over at Kieran and said, "We do."

"Yes?" Ram coaxed. "Go on."

"Well, we, um, knew both the girls who were stabbed to death. It's, uh, not something we're really proud of, but both Kieran and I ..." Colin cleared his throat again. His face was as pink as a peach. He seemed very embarrassed and nervous at the same time.

Ram sensed this and said, "Colin, I am many things, but a judge I am not, and most importantly, I am not here to look down upon you from some moral high ground. I am a homicide detective, plain and simple. And the only thing I care about more is finding out who the true killer is and bringing him or her to justice on behalf of the victims and their families. You do not realize just how important you are in helping me to solve these murders. Who you are or what you do is none of my business, but it is important that you shower me with as many details as possible, even if they seem irrelevant to the case. Details help to paint a clearer picture of the victim's life as well as those around the victim. The more you tell me, the better the chances are that a single hidden minute detail will emerge and help me to either make a break in the case or at least eliminate a suspect. Anything you confess to me that ends up being unimportant to the case, I will have forgotten, and you have my word as well as Sergeant Bartholomew Lee's that your story will never be repeated."

The men nodded that they understood. Colin, more relaxed now, continued.

"We both slept with the two girls at the same time." They both looked at Ram, who lifted his palm to continue.

"Kieran and I are what you might consider as being a couple of 'wild boys.' We like to party, wherever and whenever we can. We're both workmen's compensation lawyers over at Johnson's law offices, so we make a pretty good income, and we like to have a pretty good time to blow it on. So once Friday afternoon comes around, we are off to the bars, nightclubs, wineries, you name it. Wherever there's loud music and beautiful women, we are not very far. We party hard through the weekend until, of course, Sunday morning when you can find us at the late service over at St. John's Church. We may be bad boys, but we're Catholics, and our mothers would beat us with shillelaghs if they ever found out that we missed Mass.

"So as you can see, we work hard and party hard. And that pretty much sums up the two of us. Now as to the real reason why we're here. It's kind of revealing, Lieutenant. Anyway, we bumped into Joyce and Clara on occasions. The ladies were friends and worked with each other, so they partied together themselves a lot. One night, Kieran and I were chatting it up with the two ladies, and after a few drinks too many, we all decided to take the party to a hotel room, and there, we all had sex with each other. I mean, not altogether at the same time. I had Joyce while Kieran had Clara. Well, I wouldn't say exactly that we had them. It was pretty much the opposite. Those two ladies seemed to hold their own, and it seemed like they had us by the balls, so to speak.

"Then when we were finished, we all just laid on the beds caressing each other's bodies. After a while, I got up to take a shower, and by the time I stepped into the water, Clara had appeared from the bedroom and joined me. So we soaped each other up and down and had incredible sex while our bodies were enveloped in the steam. When we finally came out of the bathroom, Clara and I found Kieran and Joyce in the middle of their own climactic finish." Colin had to pause for a moment. Thinking back on that particular memory had caused him to shift uncomfortably in his seat.

"Anyway, we had a few more sessions just like that one; but they only happened when we all bumped into each other, and we all had that particular craving. So it was pretty random, but one time, when Joyce and I were together in the shower, I noticed a large purple bruise on her right scapula. When I asked her where she got it, she said that a crazy jealous wife clobbered her from behind. I asked who the wife was, but she just shrugged it off and said that it wasn't important. I forgot all about it because she turned to face me, and all I remembered was staring at the tiny soapy bubbles running down her breasts, round and swollen from the hot water."

Colin shivered. He closed his eyes, clearly distracted by his own reverie. Kieran nudged him back to reality, and Colin coughed. "Sorry," he said.

"Were there any other personal disagreements of any kind that Joyce revealed to you?" Ram asked. "Did she have a certain enemy or two that you could think of?"

"None at all. She was pretty closemouthed when it came to her personal life."

"How about Clara." Ram looked toward Colin then at Kieran. Both men shook their heads.

"Clara was very quiet about her personal life." This time, it was Kieran who spoke.

He said, "It was like she wanted desperately to keep her social life separate from her personal life. She could have been married for all I knew."

Ram asked Colin and Kieran a couple more questions, with Colin mostly answering them, before dismissing them. Both men got up to leave, promising to visit if they thought of anything else to reveal.

Bartholomew watched them leave and walk toward the front entrance of the police station. When the men were out of sight, he glanced back at his boss, who was busy writing something down at the desk.

"Sir?" Bartholomew asked.

"Hmm?" answered Ram.

Bartholomew's voice came out high and squeaky as he said, "Their, um, sexual trysts they just spoke of—do you think that's for real?"

"Hmm," said Ram. He looked up at Bartholomew, whose eyes remained wide with wonder. It was evident to see that the young sergeant was intrigued by Colin O'Darby's raw revelations. "It could be true. Then again, it may hold some percentage of accuracy along with some added embellishments so as to make their story more appealing. However, with the way women act nowadays, so carelessly promiscuous, I'm inclined to believe those two. They look like nice enough gentlemen despite the reckless behavior of their youthful indulgence, so I'm thinking that it was the girls who instigated their kinky experiences in the hotel rooms. Men, who are not sexual deviants, do not approach girls with the idea of having a small orgy. It's not to say that they do not enjoy it, but it's something that women have to introduce to the conversation. Aw, it's so sad to see how women allow themselves to be stripped of moral femininity."

"But to do all that with four people involved? It's like they were all swingers. What do you think about that?"

Ram looked up, amused at Bartholomew's questions. He understood the young sergeant's piqued interest. Ram said, "Being a swinger is not a crime, Bartholomew. I think that they are all young single people who acted in a reckless manner to achieve an evening's worth of sexual satisfaction. Would I have done what they did? Most likely I would not. But I believe that they were all consenting adults who wanted to enjoy something that they wouldn't normally attempt during sober circumstances. The one thing that you should remember, Bartholomew, is that although it may be crazy and fun, that short period of time could prove to cause a future of regrets. They could have all contracted some sexually transmitted disease, and don't tell me that they practiced protected sex during their trysts, especially in the shower. They could have even caused ruined relationships, or maybe even worse. Their little fun experience could have been a contributing factor in the murder of both Joyce and Clara. When it comes to murder, sex is a strong motive."

Bartholomew said, "I didn't think about that. This whole case is making me quite confused. I'm wondering, sir. Do you think that the jealous wife who bruised Joyce's back could've been Ingaborg Krause?"

"It's a good possibility," said Ram. "Mrs. Ingaborg Krause seems to be a likely person who would be angry enough to inflict such a violent wound. It looks like, Bartholomew, that we'll have to pay Rita's Roses floral shop another visit.

"Oh, goody," said Bartholomew sarcastically. He was not looking forward to another encounter with the lemon-faced Ingaborg Krause.

Chapter 11

Hans was whistling a cheery tune while he swept the floor of the floral shop. His wife, Ingaborg, came down the stairs as he was dumping the contents of the dustpan into the trash bucket. Ingaborg, tall and lean, wore a white muslin maxi dress, which accentuated the fact that she bore absolutely no feminine curves. Her snarl added to her icy appearance as if she was the replicated embodiment of a winter witch, ready to cast a spell of perpetual frost over the entire store, using nothing but one of her long bony fingers for a wand. Hans silently shuddered as he glanced over at his wife. Whatever possessed him to fall in love with such a cold woman? He dug into his mind, trying to recall from his memories, a younger single version of Ingaborg. She was a different person back then.

He met her when he was one of the groomsmen for his friend's wedding. Ingaborg was a friend of the bride and approached him with an air of charm and confidence. He remembered being smitten by her smiling face, her carefree personality, and the fact that she was of German descent. Ingaborg was great with money as well as being a savvy businesswoman. She owned her own floral shop, which was doing very well. He was impressed by her abilities of owning her own successful business at such a young age. On top of that, when Hans introduced her to his mother, a native German woman who only moved to America as a teenager, he was so proud of the fact that out of his two brothers and him, he alone had brought home a girlfriend who could converse with his mother in her native language. His mother ate Ingaborg up with a spoon. She was so happy and gushed with pride that her son, Hans, had found himself a nice German girl. So being a momma's boy, it only seemed natural that Hans simply couldn't let Ingaborg go. He had to eventually marry her, if only to please his mother.

It wasn't until a few months being married had passed when Hans was hit with the realization that he married Ingaborg for all the wrong reasons. Ingaborg had revealed her true self to be so business-like, unaffectionate, and definitely unappreciative toward anything he did for her. Ingaborg made it a point to be the one in charge, and she had no problem with giving Hans orders, but he had yet to hear a simple word of thanks from her lips. She made it a point to always be right, and the word *negotiation* was never in her vocabulary.

Before the wedding, he was so wrapped up in pleasing his mother that he didn't stop to really think about his own needs in a relationship. He also realized that although initially enamored by Ingaborg, he didn't really love her in the sense that a married man should love his wife. It wasn't like he was having any grand illusions about marriage. He realized that his wife was not always going to act and look perfect to him all the time. Weren't married men supposed to see their wives in their worst moments and still love them anyway? He wanted to love her, to be in love with her. It would be nice to do things for a woman that a man was in love with, even when it was an inconvenience to him. He wanted to be that kind of man. If only Ingaborg had even an inkling of a sweet disposition.

To be brutally frank, if Ingaborg had died, Hans wouldn't shed many, if any, tears. To make matters worse, even if she wasn't absolutely certain, Ingaborg had definitely sensed something like this in her husband. Women could sense that sort of thing, couldn't they? Cold as she was, Ingaborg was a woman. She could feel her husband's desire to pull away, and it seemed to him that because of his need to pull away, she herself had built a wall made of ice around her exterior so as to protect her own feelings from getting hurt, from feeling the pain of knowing that her husband no longer cared for her. Instead of being a heartbroken wife, Ingaborg had embraced both a defensive as well as an offensive mode of existence. Hans knew that she could have simply divorced him, but that wouldn't be good enough for her. No, Ingaborg seemed to want to punish him for not loving her. She dove into the floral business with full gusto, turning Rita's Roses into a huge moneymaker. The sacrifice for this huge success was Hans. Ingaborg hardly talked to him, and when she did, it was to point out his incompetence. Hans figured that if his wife had opened a business offering consulting advice to women on how to perform demasculinization, she'd be a millionaire by now.

And so, it was almost inevitable that Hans was driven to affairs. At first, he figured that it would just be once or twice to get it out of his system, but it wasn't long before he found himself becoming an absolute man slut. The more conquests he had bagged, the more he wanted. Hans had developed such a chronic need for sex he realized that he had become like a tiger with uncontrollable ravenous urges for meat. He would meet various women during his time delivering flower orders and would arrange times to have a rendezvous whenever and wherever convenient. There were a few times when he would have sex in the back of the delivery van. Hans had to admit, although the random intervals of intimacy were fun and noncommittal, there was a sense of unsatisfied loneliness. That was until Joyce happened.

She came into the shop one day and talked to Ingaborg. They had just finished discussing business matters together when Hans suddenly walked into the shop, back from his deliveries. His initial perception of the woman was like that of a botanist encountering a rare orchid in full bloom. Ingaborg had explained to him later that she had known Joyce since elementary school, and although she wanted to increase the business by collaborating with the event planner, Ingaborg was still a bit skeptical about Joyce's selfish and bullying nature. Hans offered to take Joyce out on his deliveries so that she could meet different potential venues, and Ingaborg, after a few hems and haws about the matter, consented.

At first, Joyce didn't give in to Hans's attempts at seduction, but after a while of talking and enjoying each other's company, the two found themselves becoming closer and closer. His time with her was actually quite fun, Hans thought. She would help Hans with his deliveries, and he would introduce her to Rita's Roses' various clients. The more business they accumulated through their method of "up close and personal" advertising, the more fun they had, and both Joyce and Hans couldn't wait for the next delivery. Finally, one day during a floral delivery to Gold Rush Winery, Joyce had obtained a big venue, which excited her so much that the two of them planned a lunch date to celebrate. They were on the road driving toward the restaurant when Hans suddenly pulled the van over to the side of the road and parked. He then climbed out of his seat, reached his hand over to cup Joyce's face and kissed her, delicately at first, then hard. Joyce responded in kind, and the two of them stayed like that for another ten minutes until Hans could no longer bear his heated desire. Hans grabbed her around the waist, and the two danced together to a song of intimate longing for each other's flesh. As he came inside Joyce, he could see that she was also climaxing, and that in its own right was a high he knew he would never recover from. They grabbed on to each other's naked body embracing that final gushing flow of rhythmic ecstasy.

After sex, the two of them had lain right there in the van for another hour, talking, laughing, and caressing. Hans ran his fingers through Joyce's dark silky hair. He traced his fingertips along the curves of her milky flesh and silently memorized each and every dark mole that added to her physical appeal. If Joyce were described as an incredible lover, it would be a gross understatement, but he also enjoyed their pillow talk. Joyce was a good listener, and she was intelligent as well. He could hear her talk about things she knew all day and never get tired of it. To be near that woman was like breathing in fresh air. Joyce was like basking in the warmth of a shining sun accompanied by a cool breeze. Since her, Hans had thought about being with no one else. Even when Joyce was busy with an event and they couldn't find time to be together, Hans had waited until she was free. He no longer had the desire to be with random girls, and what was even more enjoyable, he no longer felt lonely. She was heaven itself. Hans couldn't describe it, but he finally understood the old saying, "When you know, you know." And boy, did he know. Hans Krause had fallen in love, true love, deeply in love with Joyce Galway.

It didn't take long for Ingaborg to find out about his affair with Joyce. In a way, Hans had wanted her to know about Joyce and him. He wanted her to file for divorce and give him the freedom to pursue Joyce in a more honorable manner. But Ingaborg had different plans. Not only did she sever all business ties with Joyce, she had made certain that Hans wouldn't go anywhere without her close on his tail. In addition to keep a close eye on her husband, Ingaborg had hired a young college student to make the deliveries while Hans was subjected to the shop, tending to it and taking flower arrangement orders. Plus, Ingaborg continued to treat him with an even icier manner. It only caused Hans to feel resentful toward Ingaborg, but he also had to admit that it was his own fault. Instead of waiting for Ingaborg to file, he should be the one to step up and drive to the courthouse to fill out the necessary paperwork to start divorce proceedings. But Hans did not do that. He supposed that the reason why he didn't take the initiative was because he did feel guilty about his cheating on her.

One night, Hans had slipped a sleeping tablet into one of Ingaborg's nightly mugs of cocoa. When he was certain that she was fast asleep, he crept out of the house to seek out Joyce. It was a Saturday evening, and he knew that he might find her at one of the local social hangouts, and his luck shone when he found her car parked at the second place he looked. It was Scootin' Boots, a popular line-dancing joint where people, singles and couples, came to socialize, dance, and, of course, drink. Hans was so eager to see his dear sweet Joyce again his whole body was shaking in anticipation. But all that changed when he entered the country western nightclub and found her inside, sitting on the lap of some young cowboy. The cowboy, handsome and muscular, seemed unaffected by Hans showing up and gladly watched as Joyce walked off with Hans to talk in private. Joyce led him to a long hallway corridor called Lovers Lane where people wrote their names next to their significant other's on one of the bricks in the wall. It was there where Joyce had told Hans that their time together could never happen again. Hans couldn't believe his ears. Hadn't their time together meant anything to Joyce?

Looking back, Hans recalled how much of a fool he must have looked as he begged for her to reconsider. Joyce didn't seem to care about his pleas. Even worse, she started to argue with him. It got to the point where she was shouting at Hans with such belligerence, and he was trying to keep her voice down while getting her to continue seeing him again. She refused; it was over, she had reiterated to him, and that was that. By the time Hans had placed his hand on the exit door to the nightclub, he took one last look back. Joyce, the love of his life, he saw, had returned to her spot on the cowboy's lap, and this time, her arms were around his neck. The cowboy's muscular arms were wrapped around her small waist, and the two of them were involved in a passionate kiss. Hans recalled how his heart felt like it was being ripped in two. The inside of his chest hurt so much that he started to tear up. He had never experienced such horrible pain like that before.

Hans returned to his car and drove home in a state of absolute despair.

Chapter 12

Ram and Bartholomew drove up to Rita's Roses just in time to be almost run over by the floral shop's delivery van. A young man whose face was unknown to the detectives was driving the van.

They walked into the shop to find Hans cleaning one of the windows. Ram figured that he had already seen their vehicle and had been expecting them. Upstairs, Ingaborg's voice could be heard as she yelled down at where her husband was.

"You are such an idiot! I told you over and over again to wipe down the shower after you use it. Are you deaf or something, Hans? Do we have to make an appointment with the ear doctor for you, huh? Or maybe you can't hear me right now!" She appeared from upstairs and was clearly shocked to find the detectives present in the shop. Ingaborg's face turned pink. Ram figured that she didn't get a chance to spot his vehicle in the parking lot. It was obvious that she previously thought Hans and she were alone. Hans looked like he was enjoying his wife's embarrassment from her mistake very much.

"Hello, Mrs. Krause," said Ram, "We apologize for bothering you at such a time, but we have just a few more questions to ask you."

"Yes," Ingaborg said abruptly. Her cheeks were still pink.

"Joyce Galway had obtained a large bruise on her back, which had been the cause of an altercation. We suspect that altercation was with you."

"Why would I have an altercation, as you call it, with Joyce?"

"Because Joyce said that she was struck by a jealous wife."

"Well, that doesn't mean it was specifically me," she spat out.

"I understand, but it seems that Joyce did tell my source that the jealous wife was you, and that you had inflicted the wound," said

Ram. This wasn't true, but he figured that he might as well try a little deception to get her to confess.

Ingaborg stood still, her chiseled jaw closed tight. Hans, who was standing nearby with his arms folded over his chest said, "You attacked Joyce?"

Her eyes flashed, and she shot out lethal darts toward her husband. "Well, what do you expect?" she said. "The stupid slut was trying to steal something that belonged to me—my husband, my sweet, charming hunk of a husband!" she cried out sarcastically as if it was humorous to claim Hans as hers. Hans should have never gotten married, she had known that for a long time; but what was done was done. He was her husband, and it didn't matter what state their marriage was in. Joyce was certainly not going to swoop in and steal him away if Ingaborg had any say in the matter.

Ingaborg turned to face Ram. "That sorry excuse for a woman deserved more than a mere attack against her. Joyce Galway was a bad seed ever since she was conceived. I knew that. A lot of people knew that. I'm sure I wasn't the only wife who was angry with Joyce for using her musky scent to lure their husbands into her tangled web. Back in elementary school, she, along with a few other girls, including the other victim, Clara Morton, was known as the 'Boho Beauties.' The word *Boho* was short for Bohemian, which was sort of like a modern hippy fashion style. The girls all dressed in this type of Bohemian look. The Boho Beauties were always causing trouble for others around the school. They were a group of beauties that were also bullies, but they weren't the type of bullies who got their perfectly manicured hands dirty or dresses wrinkled. Oh no, the Boho Beauties were much too good for that. They would spread vicious rumors about people and ruin reputations on purpose just to be mean and also to let those around to know that they were number one and not to mess with their perfection, or heaven help those who would attempt such a fate." Ingaborg flung her arms about in frustration as she spoke.

"As we all got older, Joyce and her beauty pageant cronies would strut down the school hallways like it was some fashion show catwalk. At Everest High School, Joyce never had to ride the bus nor walk home because there was always some high school boy offering her a ride. She dated exactly who she wanted to, and when she became tired of one boyfriend, she'd dump him and go out with the new one the very same day. And if she wanted some other girl's boyfriend, she'd have him too while the poor girl was left behind in a heap of brokenhearted mess. I have kept myself safe from her disgusting ego-centric personality and perverted behavior throughout my childhood by simply avoiding her at all costs. Now, years later, she returns from LA hoping to make a name for herself, and here I am, thinking that time and maturity might have changed her for the better, actually consented to a business deal and maybe even a friendship with Joyce. Imagine my surprise when I find out that Joyce was back to her old tricks, and she had wanted to use my husband as her little boy toy. To make matters worse, I could see that my husband"—she shot Hans another deadly glance—"didn't just have an affair with her, he was falling in love with the dirty little slut, and I wasn't about to stand by and watch my entire life and career just crumble in such a short period of time and all for the sake of that bitch!" Ingaborg paused, realizing that she was speaking with voluminous fury. The men could see beads of perspiration glisten along the pulsating veins on her fore-head. She took a few deep breaths then continued with a calmer tone in her voice.

"Lieutenant Nandyala, you do need to understand one thing. I may have hated her, but I did not kill Joyce. You need to believe that. After I had severed all ties with Joyce, I still couldn't shake that feeling of anger toward her. So I decided to really have it out with her. All I wanted to do was to confront her about her involvement with my husband and warn her to stay away from him for good. I didn't plan on doing any sort of physical harm to her. I just wanted to give her a warning. I drove over to her house and found her in her front yard. She was planting some sort of flowers—daffodils, in fact—and there were tools lying around the place where she was working: a shovel, a spade, a gardening claw, and other relevant tools. Anyway, I said what I came to say, and I figured that would be it, and I would simply get back in my car and drive away. But do you know what she did after I told her why I was there? That little arrogant bitch simply

76

laughed at me saying that Hans was just a temporary piece that she played in her little game of men. Then she proceeded to tease me about how pathetic a lover Hans was and that I was welcome to keep him. She wouldn't stop laughing in such an evil hysterical manner as she turned her back to me. I couldn't stand it anymore. Joyce's laugh was like the sound of fingernails raking down a chalkboard. For a moment, I lost my head. I grabbed a thick branch that was lying on top of a nearby pile of firewood and cracked it over her back. Ha! It was epic. You should have seen the look on her face. She was so scared that she ran limping up the front step of her house and slammed the door shut." Ingaborg had burst out laughing so hard she was holding her stomach. When she remembered that she was admitting to an act of violence in front of police detectives, she stopped.

"That was the one and only time I did anything to her, Lieutenant, and that was also the last time I saw Joyce," she said with finality.

Hans stood there as still as stone, horrified over her revelation. He knew his wife was cold and cruel, but this was over the top. The Ingaborg he knew was harmless. She wouldn't have done anything so violent, would she? The woman before him now, confessing to such a terrible act, was sadistic. Didn't she understand that hitting Joyce could have seriously injured her, maybe even killed her? And what about Ingaborg? She could have been arrested for attempted murder or even just manslaughter. *That would be it for the business,* he thought. *Hmm,* he thought again. *There's a thought to consider, and it wouldn't be such a bad idea.* If that would be it for the business, then he would be free to divorce Ingaborg and escape from underneath her daily insults. Hans kept these thoughts to himself.

Ram coughed and said, "I have heard many different confessions in my life. I must admit that it takes a lot to get a shock out of me, and you, my dear lady, have definitely accomplished that. You have just given me a large dose to swallow, Mrs. Krause. If I didn't have the challenging task of figuring out who the real murderer is, I would have had you in handcuffs five minutes ago. However, for now, I need to focus on a few things you mentioned. You say that Clara Morton was part of this group of bullies from school days?"

"Yes," said Ingaborg.

Ram turned to her husband. "And were you, Hans, involved with Clara Morton?"

Hans's brows were furrowed in concentration. "I don't think so," he said.

"What does that mean, Hans?" Ingaborg's voice became shrill. She looked like she was ready to strangle him.

"Well, uh …" Hans closed his eyes. He had really messed up with that last answer, and his face had turned to a shade beet red. "I, uh, don't know if I did. I mean, there were so many, and I didn't catch all of their names."

Ingaborg's mouth was twisted in a disgusted manner, and her eyes were flaring. Ram placed a hand on her shoulder to restrain an outburst evidently about to happen.

"I don't think that is a good idea, Mrs. Krause. After all, you're already treading on thin ice with me. I should be cuffing you now as a good possible suspect. However, you're lucky that I don't completely believe that you are the killer of these two women.

Ram turned to Hans. "Okay, I think I understand. And you had no idea that your wife went to see Joyce at her house after she found out about the affair?"

Hans shook his head emphatically.

"And you, Mrs. Krause, didn't see Joyce again after that last encounter you just revealed to us?" Ingaborg shook her head as well. She appeared a bit calmer now.

"Okay, I believe that's all I need for the moment. Is there anything else that either of you can offer?"

Both husband and wife pathetically shook their heads, and Ram and Bartholomew left the shop. As he closed the door behind him, Bartholomew could hear Ingaborg Krause spit flaming accusations at Hans, who stood wishing that the floor would just open up and swallow him whole. Bartholomew thought to himself that if Ingaborg Krause were the last woman in the world, he wouldn't think of touching her with a ten-foot pole.

In the police vehicle, driving away, Bartholomew asked after an audible exhalation of air, "Well, sir, do you think that the wife may have stabbed Joyce, sir?"

Ram situated himself in his seat and said in a matter-of-fact tone, "No, I really meant what I said in there. However, she's got evil in her, that's for sure. And although that evil stems from all the hurt she's had to endure, she allowed it to fester inside of her all this time. I wouldn't underestimate that she's capable of doing fatal damage. That has been a strong motive for many murders throughout history, but I have a suspicious feeling that the jealousy of a scorned woman was not the real motive for these current murders. Oh, I'm not dismissing Ingaborg as a suspect, but I don't think she's a strong one in this case. That woman bleeds vinegar, and she's got a temper, but deep inside, I truly believe that she is not our killer.

"It does, however, look like both our victims are connected to Rita's Roses, the party planning business, their past as being high school bullies, and an active social lifestyle." Ram nodded.

Bartholomew asked, "So which of those places that they're both connected to holds the vital clue that leads us to their killer?"

Ram took a deep breath, then said smiling, "It's a mystery, my dear Bartholomew. It's a real mystery."

Chapter 13

Sergeant Bartholomew Lee had just sat down to enjoy a nice lunch of an egg salad sandwich mixed with chopped bacon, chips, a pickle, and a pint of ice-cold beer. He was about to take his first bite of the sandwich when the call came in. He gave his frosty mug one last longing stare before he grudgingly answered his cell phone. Ten minutes later, he was in Lieutenant Ram Nandyala's driveway ready to pick him up, and the two of them drove off in Bartholomew's car to the scene of another murder.

The house where they ended up at belonged to a Gina Sorenson. The detectives were received by forensic personnel and taken to the body. Much like the other two murders, Gina was stabbed to death; only this time, the killer made sure that an ambulance would not be necessary. The body was lying faceup on the kitchen floor. Ram could see that this woman was beautiful, even with the horrible sight of bloody wounds that had made many holes in her once perfect body. Various members of forensics were scattered about the house, taking samples, marking clues, and taking many pictures.

"Sir," an officer said to Ram, "the woman's sister is here. I had her stay in the living room. She's in a terrible state, sir."

"Thank you, Officer Greer," replied Ram.

Ram and Bartholomew went into the living room and saw a young woman, also attractive, crumpled in a ball on the loveseat. The woman's face was streaked with tears, her eyes were swollen, and her mouth was curled in depressed mourning.

"Hello," said Ram tenderly, "I'm Lieutenant Ram Nandyala. This is Sergeant Bartholomew Lee." The woman looked up to the two men. The pained expression remained on her face.

"Mary," she replied. "Mary Sorenson."

Ram sat on the sofa caddy corner to the loveseat and faced her. Bartholomew remained standing as he got out his notebook and pen, ready to take notes.

"Mary," repeated Ram, "this is a horrible time for you, and I feel very sorry for having to talk to you like this now, but questions have to be asked in order to find out who did this horrible act."

Mary sniffed, blew her nose in the little tissue she had in her hand, and nodded an understanding. Ram continued.

"Your sister, Gina. How old was she?"

"Twenty-five." Mary dabbed her eyes with the tissue.

"Did she have any enemies that you would know of?" asked Ram.

Mary nodded sadly. "A few, I guess, but none that I know of specifically. I loved my sister, Detective, but she was definitely different than me. She could be a bit reckless at times. We didn't always see eye to eye, but then again, does any sibling ever agree with the other about everything?" She giggled a little then quickly caught herself and went back to sobbing.

"What I mean is, my sister was a few years younger than me," she choked out. "So I kind of always had to look after her well-being. Growing up, she wasn't a very nice girl. I know that it's terrible of me to say, but she seemed to enjoy being a bit of a mean girl. She became friends with some girls in school who were known to gossip and spread terrible rumors about other people. It ended up being a really awful ordeal. Don't get me wrong though. Gina wasn't one to start those rumors, but she was definitely a follower, and she gravitated toward a very bad lot when it came to socializing. Gina always wanted to fit in with a group of friends, no matter how bad they were. And Joyce Galway, a fellow schoolmate of hers, was as bad as they come."

"So your sister went to Everest High School?" asked Ram.

Mary blew her nose before answering, "Yes." She nodded toward him.

"And as an adult, was Gina, ahem—still a mean girl?" asked Ram.

"Well, she wasn't after she graduated from high school, and all her friends drifted apart from each other. Oh, she'd go out and about, here and there, with different sorts of friends, but she wasn't in any trouble. That is until a year ago when Joyce Galway came back into town and got back in touch with some of her old crew, Gina being one of them. There wasn't much one could do as far as bullying goes, for that's what they were back in school—bullies. But as adults, they could do some damage. But this time, with the situation being different now that they were older, the damage was also of a different nature. They would go out on weekends and pick up various men to party with and have spontaneous wild sex. They didn't seem to care if the men were married, single, or whatever. All they seemed to care about was their own fun, having men pay for their drinks, and the crazy times spent at house parties and hotel rooms. It's a wonder that Gina didn't get a disease." Mary seemed to forget for a moment that in the next room, her sister was nothing but a lifeless corpse and that a disease would be the last of her sister's worries now.

"You know, Lieutenant," Mary said, "they used to spread pretty vicious rumors when they were younger, rumors that created scandal and damaged lives. But when they got older, it seems that they also had this desire to be the scandal. They wanted others to view them as the type who would do anything to create a bad reputation for herself. It doesn't make sense to me, but that's how they acted, like they got a high off of being bad girls."

Ram paused for a moment of reflection before asking, "Did your sister ever go to a place called Scootin' Boots?"

"Yes," said Mary. "She and I both went out there to go line dancing."

"And what about Crystal Chimes?"

"Gina did, but I didn't go. She usually went there with Joyce and some of her other friends." Mary blew her nose again and sniffed.

"I know this is a difficult question to answer, but do you know of anyone in particular who might want to stab her?"

Mary shook her head and shrugged. "Take your pick," she said. "Some jealous girl, a man who didn't like the notion of being just another forgotten notch on her designer belt. Please don't misunderstand my tone. I really do love my sister, Lieutenant, but she's dead and you need answers. Yes, I do love her, but she's never been one to follow a good group of friends. She always seemed to be driven toward unhealthy behaviors, and that kind of stuff can get girls into some serious trouble."

Ram appreciated her candid revelation to him, even though he could tell from her body language that it wasn't easy for her to admit. The poor sister had to embrace the realities of the situation, and the reality was that Gina Sorenson led a reckless sort of life and that she had most likely made a couple of enemies along the way. From the manner of death, it looked like she had made a very personal enemy. And it looked like it could be the same enemy that Joyce had.

Ram asked Mary a few more questions before they decided to leave. Both Ram and Bartholomew handed her their business cards and informed her to keep in touch if she thought of anything unusual or if she had any questions for them. She thanked them, and the detectives soon left the house.

Chapter 14

Richard Serowik was enjoying a breakfast of crispy bacon, buttered toast, poached eggs, orange juice, and strong black coffee. Morning was his favorite part of the day. He was always up early and ready to start his day off with a hearty meal, and Connie was just the type of cook to oblige him. Richard had finished the last bite on his plate and settled back in his cushioned dining chair to sip his coffee. Connie came in, took his plate, and placed the local newspaper in front of him. He thanked her and opened the pages to reveal the front cover. Written in bold font, the title "Splashed in Red" looked up at him. Interested, he proceeded to read the article.

> There is a mysterious evil haunting the Temecula Valley. It was only a month ago, the citizens of our beautiful city were able to go to bed feeling safe in the comfort of their own homes. Now, the two murders of Joyce Galway and Clara Morton that had shaken our peaceful community just a few days ago have one more horrendous killing to add to the frightening list of innocent victims: a local resident known as Gina Sorenson. First, the local country western line dancing nightclub, Scootin' Boots, was the chosen location for the killer to prey upon a poor, innocent, beautiful young woman and stab her to death. Then, to add to the horror, at another unexpected location, inside Crystal Chimes, a popular hangout for social adults, a 911 call came in regarding the stabbing of another beautiful young woman.

And now, as chilling as it sounds, the third place the killer struck was inside the safety of the victim's home. It is not known yet how the woman was stabbed, or, like the previous two killings, by whom. Gina's limp body was reportedly found lying in her kitchen, inches away from death. Medical personnel had soon arrived at the scene in hopes to save the life of the young woman. It was later reported that despite the efforts of paramedics and doctors, the young woman had succumbed to her injuries at the hospital.

Gina Sorenson was just twenty-five years old. A number of witnesses who were at each of the latest three crime scenes say that they saw no one who looked or acted suspicious in any way. It is a baffling thing to endure for everyone who is involved in some way with these murders, and many individuals have different theories as to how someone could be driven to do such a thing like murder. The most popular theory so far is that Joyce's, Clara's, and Gina's deaths could be the works of a deranged serial killer who is seeking out young beautiful women at random. Whatever the motive may be, the recent murders have been a puzzling labyrinth of complicated twists and turns that are causing homicide detectives to embark on a wild roller-coaster ride of never-ending ups and downs. In the meantime, it is in the best interest of all neighboring citizens of our community to heed to this message: Beware, Citizens of Temecula Valley. There is a killer among us, and he's targeting members of our community of the female sex, very likely our young attractive females, and if we do not practice extreme caution, any one of us or our neighbors could be next …

Richard had been so immersed in reading the article that he jumped when Margaret had entered the dining room behind him and had placed her hand on his left shoulder.

"Holy cow!" he yelped. "Margaret, you scared me. Have you seen this?" He shook the pages of the newspaper and pointed his head toward the article he was reading.

"There was another murder! It was some girl named, uh …" His eyes scanned over the article for the woman's name.

"Gina Sorensen," he said. "And she was just twenty-five years old." He let out an audible tsk-tsk. "So young, just a little older than our Cali Girl."

"Three years older," agreed Margaret. She poured herself a cup of coffee and sat down next to her husband. Her head hovered over the article. Then, suddenly, she snapped her fingers.

"I knew that name sounded familiar! If memory serves me right, she was also expected to work at the party as one of the actors. She was one of Joyce's other friends or employees or whatever. I don't know how event planners go about conducting their businesses." Margaret paused, lost in thought.

"Oh, my goodness, this is terrible! Well, you know what people say, things always happen in threes. And this is the third murder that happened. Oh dear! I can't remember exactly if she was going to be a servant or a guest at the party, but I'm pretty sure that she was a friend of Joyce's. Anyway, this is all happening so close to home. Richard, it's all such a horrendous situation, it's made me so shaky with fear especially with Halloween being just around the corner and everything spooky is in season. I can't even turn on the television without seeing some preview of a horror movie that's in theater or some sort of gory film that's running nonstop on practically every channel. That sort of thing plays with any person's mind, especially a mind that's as delicate as mine."

Margaret placed her left palm over her bosom and said, "Why, I don't even feel safe going to the grocery store."

"You hardly do go to the grocery store, Margaret. It's Connie who does most of our grocery shopping," said Richard, trying to hide the sarcasm in his tone.

"Well, I know that, Richard. It's just an expression to say that it's not safe to be out and about town until this crazy killer is caught. Oh, it gives me the willies!"

"Margaret, I don't think it's not going out that will keep you safe. Rather, it's keeping the outside from coming in that would be the more secure bet. Although it says that Gina was killed in her own home, but I'm sure that she didn't have state-of-the art security that we have here." Richard leaned back in his chair and sipped his coffee.

"That makes me wonder," he said. "Do you think that perhaps it's not safe for Calista to leave the house? I can make her stay home for a while at least. Well, I know I can't make her since she is an adult. I don't think she'd agree with me, but I do believe that we should at least ask her to stay at home."

"Make who stay home?" Calista had just walked into the room. She grabbed a clean cup and poured herself some coffee then sat in a chair next to her mother. Richard and Margaret quickly filled her in on the conversation. And just as her father had predicted, Calista exclaimed her disagreement with the notion.

Margaret said, "Honey, your father and I are simply concerned about the fact that a vulnerable beautiful young woman like yourself could be easy prey to a crazed maniac out there who is cutting women up like pieces of meat on a plate. In fact, I've been thinking—"

"Uh-oh," interrupted Calista, smiling. Her mother playfully glared at her.

"Funny, but seriously, Cali Girl, we both think it's best for you to stay home, at least for a while. Not even you can hide away from the fact that there is a deranged killer loose out there in Temecula, and he's choosing victims that seem, to me, a bit too close to home. You have to agree that something sinister is happening around here, and that it's our job as your mother and father to keep you safe."

"But what about work?" asked Calista. "It's already pretty short-staffed in the emergency room, especially after Diane went on maternity leave, and they can't replace her with anyone else in the emergency unit just yet. Nobody else likes the idea of working the graveyard shift, which was her shift. So you see, I have to go back to work. I have today and the next three days off so that'll be fine, but

I'll have to return. Plus, I have a date tonight, so I'll have to leave the house anyway."

"A date! How exciting. With whom?" The idea of her daughter having a date seemed to cause Margaret to completely forget about Calista's safety and to focus on her daughter's love life.

"One of the firemen who wheeled in the two murder victims into the ER while I was working. He gave me his number and I called him. We're going to Collette's for dinner," Calista said beaming.

"Calista, I don't think that's such a good idea. There's been another murder, a third one," her father said.

Calista looked shocked. "No, there wasn't! You're joking. Seriously?" she asked.

"It's right here." Richard pointed to the article as he passed the paper to his daughter. Calista took it in one hand and, with the other, grabbed a slice of whole wheat toast. She took a bite of the toast and tasted the salted butter that had already been spread evenly over it. Calista smiled with satisfaction. From simple to gourmet, Connie always knew exactly what to serve and when. After she read the entire article, Calista drained her coffee in just a few gulps. *This is insane,* she thought. She looked over at her mother as she returned the paper to her father.

"Mom, I know that you place your heart and soul into this event like no one I've ever seen in my life, but don't you think that the three murders is reason enough to cancel the party? There also could be danger due to the connection that we have to the victims? You know that you'd have to consider that."

"Shut your mouth, young lady!" Margaret said. Her palm went back to her bosom. "Don't even speak of such things. Murder or no murder, I am determined to host this. It's not just a party, it's so much more than that. It's an event that provides entertainment remembered by our guests in the months after."

"Margaret," Richard interjected, "Calista does have a point. We can always do it next year, and please don't be so dramatic about it. This is murder we're talking about, Margaret, my dear." Richard placed a comforting hand on his wife's. Margaret gave him a despondent glance that told him she did not find that idea at all agreeable.

He knew all about his wife's little funny quirks, especially her stubborn ones, and he understood how much Margaret's parties meant to her. They gave her this pleasurable sense of creating something entertaining to others. His wife thrived on big projects where entertainment was concerned, and hosting a party in a mansion as large as theirs was a massive project in itself. To cancel it would force Margaret to undergo a week or two of gloom, and that was something that Richard wanted to avoid. He loved Margaret, but she could take negativity to the point of overexaggeration and cause the entire household to experience emotional turmoil.

So in an attempt to provide some means of negotiation, Richard said, "If you are dead set on having the party, then there must be a way to have it and not have to worry about any potential danger. *Any potential danger.*" He looked with meaning toward his wife.

Margaret perked up. "How about a team of security? Isn't Mike Paget the head of the, um, Parkway Security Company?" she suggested.

Richard nodded thoughtfully and said, "I suppose I could hire a few guys to keep an eye on the place. Plus, you should hire a party planner that you've already used in the past to manage the party. That way, we know exactly who we're getting this year."

"Already ahead of you, Dickey Dear," said Margaret, using her little pet name for him when she was extremely happy. "And we can still have the murder mystery theme! So far, I've ordered all the types of food and drink, and the decorators are coming next week to transform this entire home into a vintage-looking haunted mansion. It'll be like stepping into the past. I've also ordered our costumes. You are going to enjoy your character, Richard. I've ordered a Hercule Poirot costume for you, and it's going to look absolutely authentic!"

"Mm, sounds promising. Do I have to grow a mustache for the evening?" asked Richard.

Margaret waved that notion away and said, "Oh no. I've already ordered you a fake mustache with Poirot's trademark design. By the way, Cali Girl, you need to choose a costume quickly. I didn't order one for you because you didn't tell me what you are going to be."

Calista had finished her toast and was busy licking the butter off her fingers. "I already know what I'm going to be. Do you think that you can guess what my costume is?" she asked.

"Sister Teresa of Calcutta!" a voice boomed from outside the dining room. Richard, Margaret, and Calista all turned to watch the final member of their little immediate family enter the room. Behind him, a very tired Jason Thompson followed, clearly in need of some richly strong caffeinated brew and an aspirin. Jason had been Connor's best friend since grade school. Jason had decided to attend nursing school, and he was in the final stages of his education. Although he was busy with school and his internship at the hospital, Jason had frequently made time to paint the town wild with Connor. They would usually drink until they couldn't stand any more, order a taxi, and pass out in Connor's parents' pool house, which was a fully furnished cabin next to the outdoor swimming pool. There had been many a two-in-the-morning appearances of the glow of taxi lights at the Serowik mansion, and all due to those two boys; and sometimes, although Margaret should never find out, some girls. They would all stumble out of the taxi, and once the driver was given a much too generous tip, they would scamper down the walkway, giggling and stumbling into trees and bushes toward the pool house. The little cabin was the best location to sleep off a night of wild fun since no one inside the main house would have to undergo disruption of sleep.

"Well, good morning to you two boys," Richard said, amused by the sight of their red eyes and the evident stagger in their steps. He was used to the bushel-filled wild oats still alive and kicking within his son, and even though he understood a young man's need to let loose and have fun, Richard had deeply wished that Connor would soon mature and take life seriously. He wanted for Connor to make a career for himself like his daughter had done. After all, he wasn't going to support his son forever. He had already supported him long enough and would have cut Connor off a long time ago. However, Margaret had something to say about that. Her compassion for their son had gone so far as to baby the man. And Richard, never enjoying engaging in argument with his wife, allowed his wife to excuse Connor's reckless behavior.

"Hi, Dad, Mom," Connor said and bent down to plant a kiss on his mother's cheek. Both young men joined the rest of the family and began filling their plates with bacon, eggs, and toast. Connor and Jason took turns passing Tabasco sauce, salt, and pepper back and forth. They ate heartily and, much to the cook's delight, grabbed seconds.

Calista said, "There's been a third murder, and it's connected to the first two. Gina Sorensen was a friend of the first two stabbing victims who were wheeled into my unit while Erin and I were working."

Jason coughed. "Erin, huh? How's she doing?"

"Oh, she was a bit shaken by the fact that the women who were wheeled past her had just experienced their flesh being torn through by a jutting knife just minutes earlier."

Margaret shuddered with audible disgust. "Please, Cali Girl, not while we're eating."

Connor continued to shovel his breakfast into his mouth. He did not seem disgusted in the least. Richard, who was constantly fantasizing about his son with a job, was thinking that Connor would make a good butcher.

Jason asked, "Are you still having your Halloween party, Mrs. S.?"

Calista nodded. "We were just talking about which costumes we would pick out," she said, "and I don't think I'm going as a nun." She looked pointedly at her brother, then added, "I want to dress in something a little more, um, provocative." She whispered the last word even though it was obvious that everyone heard it, including her father.

Richard rolled his eyes and added, "Much to my distress."

"Oh, Dad, it won't be that bad." Calista shot her father an innocent grin.

"Cali Girl has a little boyfriend!" Margaret gushed.

"Oh, really?" said Connor, amused. "And what does this little boyfriend do?"

Margaret answered before Calista could speak, "He's a hot fireman!"

"Mom!" Calista said with a pout in her voice. Her cheeks were pink with embarrassment.

"Aw, a fireman. Anyone I know?" asked her brother. "Although I don't really know any firemen." He picked up his glass of orange juice and drank.

"I don't think so," said Calista. "And he's not my boyfriend. I hardly know him, except for the fact that his name is Fitz and he works at one of the fire stations here in town. We're going on a first date tonight, so wish me luck."

"Why don't you invite him to the Halloween party?" asked Margaret.

"Yes," Connor chimed in, "let him see what a nice and normally dysfunctional family we are, up close and personal."

"Well," said Calista thoughtfully, "let me see how the date is first, and if all goes well, I'll invite him."

"Erin's coming to the party, right?" Jason asked eagerly.

"Of course!" said Calista, "Erin seems more excited about the party than I am. She has been so excited to show off her character as a sexy wicked witch from the *Wizard of Oz* costume. Of course, we're matching since I'm going to be a sexy Dorothy." She shot a sideways glance over at her father and said, "Well, not too sexy. My gingham dress will be a little short. I'll have a pair of lacy thigh-high tights and sparkly red shoes. I even have this cute little stuffed dog that looks exactly like Toto peeking out of a handheld picnic basket."

Richard pushed his chair back from the table and got up to leave. He had read enough of the newspaper to be satisfied, so he handed it over to his wife, who gratefully accepted.

Calista drained her own cup and followed her father out of the room, leaving Margaret alone with her brother and his best friend. She could hear them eagerly chatting about their plans for the day.

Chapter 15

Early the next morning in the Temecula Valley Morgue, Lieutenant Ram Nandyala and Sergeant Bartholomew Lee were standing over the body of Gina Sorensen. Her corpse was as still and as white as a marbled statue created by an expert sculpture artist who used a mixture of violent death and beauty as inspiration. Gina was such an attractive woman. He could see that from the photos displayed around her house, as well as those that her sister had shown him. From her lovely flowing red hair down to her perfectly pedicured toes, the woman was a vision of youthful vitality. She must have possessed a fiery personality. *And now,* Ram thought to himself, *someone took that vitality from her in a most evil manner. Poor girl, she must have undergone an absolutely terrifying ordeal.* The killer had rammed the knife inside her body over and over again, tore her vital organs apart with angry thrusts, and forced her lungs to fight for one more inhalation, knowing all too well that it would be an impossible feat.

The medical examiner, a small, thin, mousy-looking man known as Dr. James Walsh gave a quick summarized report regarding the details of the patient, the cause of death, and a few other pieces of information that he felt might be important for the detectives to know.

"From the wounds," Dr. Walsh explained, "I was able to note that they were all made with the same knife, which had a smooth edge. The thrusts were clean, but not professional. I don't think that the killer knew exactly which areas of the body would prove fatal. I think that the killer was just haphazardly stabbing at anywhere on the victim's body. It looks like the killer initially punctured the throat first, which would have rendered the victim helpless for the rest of the stabs. The throat wound is at an upward angle toward the victim's brain stem, so I ascertain that the killer was shorter than her. Of course, Ms. Sorenson was wearing high heels, which would make the killer seem much shorter than he or she is in real life. After I measured her and added in the length of the heels, Ms. Sorenson's height would have been five feet, ten inches when she was killed. Calculating the angle of the wound and subtracting the heels, I can roughly estimate the killer's height to be five feet, six inches. Since there are no defensive wounds on the victim, I figure that she was immediately immobilized once the killer started the attack. It almost seems like the victim was having a friendly or at least a civilized conversation with the killer and was surprised by the sudden attack."

"Five feet, six inches," repeated Ram. "That could be a really short man. However, it almost seems probable that we're looking for a woman."

"That does seem to make more sense," agreed the medical examiner. "Oh, and I also reviewed the other two victims' wounds, and they all have that same puncture wound in the neck at around the same angle as this one here, so I'm thinking that you're looking for the same killer in all three cases."

When they left the morgue, Ram and Bartholomew decided to return to Ram's office to review their notes before questioning anyone else just yet. A portfolio containing all of Gina's personal information sat on Ram's desk, most likely left by one of the officers. He opened the folder and perused the contents along with Bartholomew peeking over his shoulder. Gina Sorensen was the same age as Joyce and Clara, she went to the same schools, worked under Joyce during some events, and, according to Gina's sister, Mary, Gina frequented the same night scenes as Joyce.

"Let me guess," Bartholomew joked, "Gina was also known as one of the infamous bully Bohos."

"Boho Beauties, and it does look that way, doesn't it," Ram said. "She was a mean beauty and a friend of Joyce Galway, besides being Joyce's coworker. She's also the same age as Joyce. If these women had a lot in common, they probably slept around, perhaps with the same men. There definitely seems to be many connective ties among these women. The only problem that we are faced with is the true reason why these women are being stabbed. Are their deaths the result of some type of vengeance conducted by one of their past victims? Could it be their promiscuous nature today?"

"You mean like some moral avenger is ridding the world of its promiscuous filth, one beautiful slut at a time?" asked Bartholomew.

Ram shook his head and said, "I don't think that this has to do with anything formal or random. Plus, a woman's sexual prowess is her own business, and there are too many promiscuous people, male and female, to make a difference in the world by killing just three."

"What if three is just the beginning?"

"True," said Ram, "but the fact that these three women are related in both a personal and professional manner is making me realize that the motive behind their deaths is a personal one. In fact, I think that it's someone whom they all knew, and possibly were friendly with, making it easier to stab them without them foreseeing the attack. If you think about it, all of their stab wounds are located in the front of their bodies, meaning that they had to look their attacker in the eyes and feel the hate as they were dying."

"That's a pretty good theory, and you're most likely dead on, but we can't rule out any other possibilities."

"When have you ever known me to rule out anything during a case, Bartholomew?"

"Oh, never," agreed Bartholomew. "Sorry, I meant that for my own personal notes and was just thinking out loud."

Ram smiled. Sergeant Lee had been working with Ram for years. Bartholomew did not look like he was a match for the tall, lean, copper-toned lieutenant. In contrast, Bartholomew was about medium height for a man. Around his girth, he held a bit of a pudgy frame that would only get worse if he didn't control his intake of fattening food. Bartholomew did enjoy his hamburgers and hot dogs served by a local diner conveniently located a block away from the police station. However, despite his outward appearance, Bartholomew was a perfect fit for Ram. He was not only brilliant and intuitive, but he also had a strong sense of loyalty and integrity. Plus, Bartholomew still displayed signs of insecurity. This was the main reason why Ram wanted to work with him on homicide cases. Bartholomew might be a great asset to solving murders, but he was not born with a single conceited or arrogant bone in his body, which meant that he was open to the lessons that Ram was willing to teach. Plus, Bartholomew was the only officer in the entire precinct who didn't act as though he felt awkward around Ram's daily indulgences.

Ram was an avid believer in the powers of yoga, which he practiced daily. Anyone who entered his office was met with a relaxing melody of meditation music and the sweet aroma of incense. His daily ritualistic indulgence included that of Indian and Chinese tea, his meditation music playing nonstop, and his incense. It "relaxes the mind and rejuvenates one's body," Ram often said. Although Bartholomew did not practice Ram's lifestyle, he accepted and respected it.

"Tell you what, Bartholomew," said Ram decidedly, "why don't we each take a possible lead and work on it. If it doesn't seem to go anywhere, we can choose another to follow."

"I've got dibs on a jilted lover," said Bartholomew, "even though it'll probably be a dead end. It looks like we're definitely looking for a woman."

Ram said, "Very well, then I'll take the theory of a jealous girlfriend or wife. But first, I'd like to have a few more conversations with some of the medical staff at Serowik hospital who came in contact with the first two victims during the final minutes of their lives."

Before they left, the two detectives agreed on a time to reconvene and to share notes the following day.

Ram took his own car, a 2014 Mercedes-Benz CLS550, and let Bartholomew have the unmarked police vehicle.

Chapter 16

Mary had been sitting alone in her sister's home. She thought about Gina, her bloody body lying in the kitchen, and it made her sick to think about it. She never liked her sister, that was true. Gina had such a selfish disposition, always looking at herself in the mirror and admiring her reflection. Ever since she was little, Gina had made it a point to wear flashy outfits, and they always had to be put together to match her liking. Whenever they were out shopping with their mother, Gina would choose an item, usually an expensive one, and if their mother said no, Gina would stomp and pout until her mother would finally give in to her daughter's tantrums. Mary had never understood this about her sister, since Mary herself had always settled for whatever her mother had picked out for her. She didn't even think that Gina had good taste in clothes. Gina was attracted to washed-out denims and neon colors. She also enjoyed piling on layers and layers of different clothing to the point of unnecessary fashion. That didn't even count the makeup Gina would wear. It was embarrassing for Mary to see her sister's face transformed into a clown's dream. Mary thought her sister looked ridiculous all the time, especially since Mary had enjoyed dressing in solid earthy colors, nothing too bright and flashy, and she had only worn natural-looking tones on her face. In school, no one would ever guess that they were sisters, except for the red hair.

Although the differences between her and her sister had caused a barrier in between them all these years, Mary would never have wished such a horrible death upon her sister. In fact, she wouldn't wish such a death on anyone, including her worst enemy. In order to spare her mother and father the painstaking job of gathering Gina's personal property, Mary had volunteered to do it. She also wanted to help

Lieutenant Ram Nandyala in his investigation of her sister's murder, so it was going to take some time to accomplish all that she wanted to do. She wanted to search around the house for something, anything that may possibly point to the reason why Gina was killed. There had to be a reason, right? Gina couldn't have been a random pick.

Mary looked around Gina's room for anything that might be useful to give to the police. She couldn't see anything promising, just the normal bedroom contents: bed, nightstand, dresser, vanity, and closet. The bed still had clothes on it. Mary figured that all of Gina's clothes and shoes could be donated to a local thrift shop. She lifted the pillows that were on top of Gina's bed. Underneath was a large hardbound book. Mary picked it up and read the front. It was a 2005–2006 yearbook of Everest High School, Gina's yearbook. Mary tried to recall what grade Gina was in during this year. *Gina was a freshman,* she thought. Mary opened it and sifted through the pages. There was nothing that stood out among the pages. The contents were only the usual notes signed by other fellow students wishing Gina well and jotting down phone numbers to keep in touch. She also saw the photos of the staff and saw that there were drawings of devil's horns, mustaches, and other crazy props on their portrait photos. Most likely it was Gina who drew these extra features on the staff members she least liked. Mary wondered why her sister had felt a need to get out her yearbook. It was curious. She wondered if she should tell the lieutenant of this. It seemed like such an insignificant action. People often had moments when they felt nostalgic and wanted to look through their old yearbooks, and that was what Gina most likely felt recently. But then again …

Mary went to the garage to look for a cardboard box or something that could store a bunch of stuff. She found a plastic bin, and on the side of the bin, she wrote the following in permanent marker: *EVIDENCE???* She figured that whatever she found could also be construed as just regular stuff owned by a young single woman and have absolutely no relevance to the case, but Mary felt that if she could provide at least just one clue that would help lead the police in the right direction of the killer, then she could rest easier knowing that she helped bring her sister's killer to justice.

Chapter 17

Calista was sitting on her bed, reading a book and thinking about the recent murders that happened. *Does this all have anything to do with us?* she thought to herself. *Are these murders happening by someone involved with the same company as the victims?* Was the killer one of the hired actors who took this opportunity to kill, using the party as an ominous palette to paint a picture of murder? It was Halloween after all, time for ghosts and witches and scary stories. She just hoped that the murderer wouldn't succeed in killing this year's Halloween party as well, if only for the sake of her mother's feelings. Calista had to admit that this would be such a bummer. Calista did not condone the act of snuffing someone's life out, but she also didn't want a killer to end a family tradition that quite a few people had looked forward to. Her mother really did throw fantastic parties, and even though Margaret Serowik did not completely organize them on her own, she made sure to hire the very best help, and the results were nothing short of fabulous. People from all over the city would kill to be invited.

Wait! Maybe the killer is someone who never got an invitation. Oh, Calista, she thought to herself, *you really are a silly imaginative girl!*

Most importantly, she didn't want to voice these concerns, silly or serious, to her mother. *Poor Mom,* she thought, *can't take this kind of stress, especially with her bad heart.* So Calista talked to her best friend and coworker, Erin, who was actually a big help. It always felt good to talk about things that confused one, even if talking didn't exactly solve anything.

A knock on her door interrupted her thoughts. Genevieve, one of their maids, came in to collect Calista's laundry. Calista jumped from her bed to her hamper. She gathered all the clothes in her arms and handed them to her family's maid, thanking her. Although Calista did her own laundry, sometimes Genevieve would take Calista's clothes if she didn't have enough to fill up the washing machine.

Calista looked down at her watch. It was almost time for her shift at the hospital to begin. She yawned, stretched her arms, and proceeded to dress in her scrubs.

Although challenging, her job at the hospital did not seem too harrowing. After she arrived, she saw that the emergency room was not as busy as usual, so she and Erin could enjoy a few words with each other in between their rounds with the patients. Calista was so happy that she had her friend there as a coworker. Erin seemed to share Calista's desire for competency on the job. They showed up early to work, they both never took advantage of the sick days they had, and during their shifts, the hours seemed to run smoothly. The time also went fast since the girls had each other for amusement, and there never seemed enough time to engage in gossip.

"So, Calista, you got to go out with the hot fireman!" Erin gushed when Calista told her about her dinner date the evening before. Calista beamed and blushed while she nodded her excited consent. Erin squealed in delight then demanded details.

"How was it?" she asked. "How was he?" Erin raised her eyebrows.

"It was wonderful, dinner was delicious, and he"—Calista stared knowingly at her friend—"was a perfect gentleman."

"Oh, you likey," Erin teased. "Well, what's not to like? He is a cutie."

Calista gave Erin a look of sheepish affirmation, which made the two nurses burst into giggles.

"And what are you girls so happy about," a voice belonging to Dr. Neville Williams called out, prompting Calista and Erin to turn to him.

"Calista was just telling me about a potential boyfriend," said Erin.

Dr. Williams looked crestfallen, but he said, "Well, then I'm sorry to interrupt your conversation." He walked away.

Both Calista and Erin remained silent watching him wander off with his head down. Calista turned to her friend. "Erin, you shouldn't have said that."

"Why not," Erin retorted. "You can date whomever you wish, and Dr. Neville could have asked you out a while ago, but he didn't. Instead, he spent his time flirting with other females in this hospital, not to mention all the girls he's winked at outside work. He has no right to look depressed upon hearing that you have found yourself a nice little fireman. Dr. Williams was acting like you were expected to wait for him."

"You're right," agreed Calista. "I always suspected that he was a little bit interested in me, but in a way I always knew that I wasn't the only one he was laying his charms on."

"Oh, he was interested in you, but he has this air about him that says he's God's gift to women, and you really don't want a man like that. Unfortunately, a lot of doctors have that kind of self-view. Let's say he did ask you out, you dated, became boyfriend and girlfriend, and made it official. He still wouldn't change his personality. It might take him a few months, but he'd be back to his old charming ways of flirtation. If you ask me, I'd set my sights on someone a bit more reliable. And if that fireman turns out to be less than honest when it comes to relationships, then I'd tell you to not waste your time on him either."

Calista smiled. "You're a good friend, you know that, Erin? I can always count on you to speak candidly with me."

"That's what best friends are supposed to do," said Erin, cradling Calista's shoulders with one arm.

Dr. Williams had finished with some of his patients' postoperative care then he returned to his office to finish some paperwork. He did not enjoy filling out forms. The space to print was so small, and one was expected to write legibly so that others reading the form could make out the words. Didn't people know that doctors have bigger things to worry about than worrying about their penmanship? It seemed to him as a tedious waste of his professional talents. He wondered if he could get a medical transcriptionist to fill out all of his documents for him. That would help him out a lot. Dr. Williams made a mental note to ask the hospital coordinator how he would go about obtaining a person to do his secretarial work. A knock on his office door was a welcome interruption from his work.

"Come in," he called out. He stretched his arms above his head and yawned. He couldn't wait for this shift to end.

Lieutenant Ram Nandyala peeked his head in through the door. "Sorry to bother you, Doctor, but I came from the station and am curious about a few things. I hope you can clear them up for me."

"Of course, Detective. Please have a seat." Dr. Williams gestured to his chair, which Ram took, and for a moment, the two men faced each other. Ram knew how delicate of a matter this was to discuss, even as a professional, so he reviewed a number of ways to word his questions before he met the hospital surgeon.

"I am wondering," Ram began, "about the second and third victims who also succumbed to fatal stab wounds recently." Dr. Williams nodded for Ram to proceed.

"I know that I talked to you about Joyce Galway, but we never got a chance to discuss the other two victims, Clara Morton and Gina Sorensen. Were you involved at all with those women?"

Dr. Neville Williams sat up in his chair. "No, I was never involved, in the personal sense, with them. However, I did know them. Clara and Joyce hung out a lot, and yes, sometimes Gina would join them during their ladies' nights. As far as I knew Gina and Clara, it was pretty informal, like a 'Hi, it's nice to meet you' sort of situation. We would exchange pleasantries whenever we would bump into each other, but it never went much further than that. I knew more about them through talking to Joyce. Joyce enjoyed only one subject, and that was herself, but occasionally, she would let me know a few things about other people she knew, including Clara and Gina."

"I see. And did she tell you anything that may seem important to me in finding their killer? Did they have a common enemy? Was there any kind of scandal that hung among the three women, or even just two of them?"

"None that I can recall, except for the fact that all three were absolute sluts," said Dr. Williams. "I'm sorry. I know that's harsh, but as you say, there's been three murders, and if people who knew them are absolutely truthful about who they were while they were alive and what their personalities were like, then there may be a possible breakthrough."

Ram smiled. "I'm glad you see it that way too. So is there anything that you noticed that may seem relevant?"

Dr. Williams thought to himself for a moment. He placed his fingers on his forehead as if digging deep within his mind for something, anything to offer." Then all of a sudden, he snapped his fingers and spoke slowly, trying to recall each detail.

"When I wheeled Gina in the operating room, she was delirious from the morphine that they injected her with in the ambulance, and she was saying a bunch of things through her drunken stupor. Anyhow, I did hear her mutter something about someone named Gloria."

"Gloria?" repeated Ram. "Are you sure that's the name she said?"

Dr. Williams squinted his eyes. "Yeah, pretty sure, but you've got to remember how chaotic it was that night, and I was so busy preparing for the operation that I couldn't figure out anything else she was saying. In fact, I don't even know if I recalled the name 'Gloria' correctly."

"It's definitely something to go on for the moment," said Ram. "Do you know who wheeled her in? If I can talk to them, maybe they'll have caught something else that Gina said."

"Of course. In fact, I think they're in the emergency unit as we speak. Their names are Nurses Erin Carney and Calista Serowik."

Ram smiled. "I have gotten to know Calista quite well during this investigation. Well, Doctor, if you think of anything else in the future, please do not hesitate to call me. You do not know how important even the slightest insignificant detail can be to an investigation." Ram got up to leave. Dr. Williams agreed and gave his sincere promise that he would call if there were anything further to report.

Ram made his way to the emergency unit, when he spotted the nurse named Erin. He stopped her in the hallway.

"Ms. Erin?" Ram asked.

"Yes?" said Erin, squinting at him. "Oh, you must be the detective that Calista has been talking nonstop about! It is so nice to meet you." Erin shook his hand eagerly.

"Lieutenant Ram Nandyala," said Ram. "It is very nice to meet you. I hate to make this short, but I do have to visit a lot of people in order to conduct quite a few inquiries. You understand?" Erin nodded excitedly.

"I understand that you helped to wheel in the recent stabbing victims on the two separate occasions." Again, Erin nodded.

"Did you notice anything about either victim that may help to point me in the correct direction of the killer? Anything on the victim or something the victim said that seemed out of the ordinary?"

At first, Erin shook her head, but then she paused. "There was something odd about the second victim, Clara," she started to say, then stopped, thinking to herself.

"Yes," coaxed Ram.

"She was on the gurney when we were wheeling her in, and she was trying to toss and turn, mumbling a bunch of stuff out loud. None of it seemed to make any sense."

"Do you remember any of her words?" asked Ram.

"Yeah, she said something like, 'It wasn't me, it was all Joyce's fault. She, it wasn't me. It wasn't—Gloria, Gloria did this. It was Gloria!' And soon, like a maniac, she was shouting the name Gloria, saying that it was her who did this. By the time we sent her through the double doors to the operating room, she was too much out of earshot for us to hear anything else. That, to me, seemed pretty odd. But I just thought that she was delirious from being attacked, mixed in with the morphine injections. It was all a lot for her to endure at once. Anyway, that's all that seemed out of the ordinary, other than the time when Calista found the first victim's boots in the emergency unit along with that note."

"Thank you, Erin. You've helped me out more than you know." Ram handed her his business card and walked away, leaving behind a beaming Erin, evidently proud of her contribution to his case.

Erin stood still, staring at the card in her hand. She reveled in her pride for a moment more, then she skipped off to her nurses' station where Calista was busy filling out paperwork. She burst out the details of the conversation she had just had with the lieutenant with her best friend.

Chapter 18

Ingaborg had been spritzing some flower arrangements around her shop with a light mist of water from a handheld spray bottle. The expression on her face was like a spoiled raisin, pinched and sour. The flower shop, Rita's Roses, was an absolute success, thanks to her quick mind and skill with figures. If only she had made smart decisions when it came to love. *Love! Ha,* she scoffed to herself. On the outside, Hans was a good choice. He was tall, handsome, and had this charming personality that could influence anyone to do anything for him. Well, almost everyone. Although he had successfully influenced her into falling in love with him long ago when they first met each other, his powers of charm had failed to make her fall back in love with him.

Ingaborg was blonde with milky white skin, but her thin, frail appearance did not follow the usual stereotype attached to the outward-looking characteristics of her features. Ingaborg was a strong woman who could endure—and had endured—much. She was not an idiot—far from it, in fact. Plus, she had good common sense, which allowed her to realize long ago exactly what Hans was up to with those random floozies he had rendezvous with in the back of the van as well as other places. She began to sense something wrong when Hans seemed a little too eager to make the flower deliveries, so she followed him a couple of times to where he had his trysts. She used to sit in the driver seat of her car, seething with fury as she watched the van rock back and forth from the motion of the two bodies engaged in amorous sex. But she never let on that she knew anything, so the knowledge sat within her like a sickening pool of bile.

She hated Hans, *really* hated him. What made it all so terrible was that it hurt her. Ingaborg's heart felt as though it was ripped apart, stripped into tiny little pieces until there was nothing left to repair or feel any small semblance of love. All that remained in her breast was a smoky cloud of passionate hate for the man who had robbed her of any sort of happiness. *Well, two could play at that game,* she thought. And she could play it better. Ingaborg had decided to spend every day making Hans's life a living hell, so much so that he would be forced to either divorce her or kill her. At that point, Ingaborg didn't care what he did. She didn't care even if she lived or died. She just wanted to make sure that he suffered equally as much as she did. She wanted his heart to rip as hers did. She wanted Hans to be deprived of a woman's warm touch and affection and replaced with the cold icy sting of her sharp words of degradation at him.

A tear trickled down her cheek, and she quickly wiped it away, furious at herself for showing any outward sign of vulnerability. She was not going to feel or show any sort of weakness. That was for certain. If she did, then she was afraid that she might crumble, and she couldn't have that, could she?

From the moment Hans had begun being unfaithful, she had let him think that his little amorous meetings had gone around her radar and that she had no clue as to his goings-on. They had a business to run, and if she didn't manage it correctly, it could mean the end of the floral shop, so she couldn't let herself be distracted by their own domestic drama. She had driven herself into the business to the point where all she worried about was making more and more money, and she succeeded in doing so. Ingaborg had even set up a private account that Hans had not known about. Little by little, she dropped deposits into it so that it would go unnoticed. This was also her little act of revenge against him. He could have his sleazy affairs while she had her secret bank account.

That is until the day Joyce Galway had walked into Rita's Roses. At first, Joyce had appeared to be a changed person. She embraced Ingaborg warmly, and they had talked a little about the old times. Joyce had even admitted that she wasn't the nicest person in school, which made her seem even more believable. Joyce even apologized for any hurt that she may have caused Ingaborg. Ingaborg figured that it was a good step toward a positive change in Joyce. She didn't completely trust her, but Ingaborg was an adult with a business to run; and when they talked about their two businesses working together, Ingaborg was immediately on board. One could never have too much business, and having a highly regarded party planner as one's connection for floral venues was a definite plus.

For the first month, Joyce seemed to be the perfect business partner. There were charity events and weddings at the wineries. There were corporate parties that required some embellishments to the party's ambience. There were even personal parties at some rich mansions that entertained over fifty guests. Whatever venue she had, Joyce always put Ingaborg in charge of floral arrangements. They were making money hand over fist. She and Ingaborg kept in close contact, and there didn't seem to be a single problem. That is until Hans came into the picture. As soon as he offered to take Joyce out with him during his deliveries so that she could possibly expand her client list, Ingaborg suspected that he would put the moves on her. But she wasn't so sure about Joyce at that time. Joyce had seemed so refined, so well put together. On the outside, she was this lovely woman in possession of perfect standards of morality, loyalty, and integrity. On the inside, Ingaborg soon realized, Joyce was nothing but a cheap slut!

To make matters worse, for Ingaborg had forced some semblance of acceptance to Hans's scandalous nature, Hans fell deeply in love with Joyce. Ingaborg knew it. She knew it in her bones. That look on his face was evident. Leaving for their trysts was not just exciting for Hans. There was something else there, something in the undercurrent of his manner. It wasn't just lust. Lust was carnal, shallow. No, this was more than that. This thing he had with Joyce meant something to him. Ingaborg hated to admit it, but Joyce was very special to Hans, and she could tell that he was slipping away, body and soul. Unless she took hasty action, Ingaborg was going to lose her husband for good.

That brought about another idea to her mind. Could Hans have killed Joyce out of ... out of what? There wasn't a real motive for him killing Joyce. Ingaborg knew that Hans was crestfallen after she put a stop to their affair, but wouldn't that prompt him to kill her instead of Joyce? It would seem probable that he would get rid of his wife in order to pave the way for Joyce and him. But Ingaborg wasn't dead, and Hans didn't seem like the type who would kill anyone. No, Hans had the mousy type of personality who would cower away in a world of secrets and lies rather than openly murder someone. Ingaborg should know, being married to him. In fact, she was more of a killer than Hans was.

Ingaborg sighed and finished spraying the plants. She glanced over at the clock to see what time it was; 12:05 p.m. Lunch should be ready.

"Hans!" she called out. "Have you got those sandwiches ready?"

"They're on the table, dear!" she heard him shout back with a tone of mocked reverence.

Ingaborg ate her sandwich in silence. It was her favorite: sliced chicken, tomato, lettuce, mustard, salt, and pepper. She wondered what she was going to dress up as, at the Serowiks' Halloween party. They were hired by Margaret Serowik to provide the floral arrangements, and Ingaborg had already planned on filling the house with plenty of oranges, browns, reds, and yellows to fit in with the seasonal theme. *It should look really good,* she thought, munching away at her lunch. Hans already had his costume. He was going as Thor. *Ugh,* thought Ingaborg. He would take the opportunity to show off his blond hair and toned body. It was a good thing that Thor's character was not shirtless. She glared at nothing in particular as she bit down furiously at her sandwich. She would think up a good costume, she thought, something really good to match her emotional state of being. What was her state of emotions? She felt angry, that's for sure. She couldn't remember a moment lately when she didn't feel that toxic negativity coursing through her veins. If she was exhausted from feeling so much anger, Ingaborg had become numb and devoid of any emotion.

Then she realized what she should go to the party as. *Yes,* she thought with a devilish grin on her face. *That would be perfect for me.* Ingaborg had decided to go to the Serowiks' party dressed as the Ice Queen.

Chapter 19

Sergeant Bartholomew Lee was sitting in the office of Kieran Ryan, asking questions and taking as many notes as his hand could write. Kieran was a bit more forthcoming now than he was when both Colin and he paid a visit to the police station. It seemed that in his own office, Kieran was able to feel more at ease. Kieran's office was equipped with a large mahogany desk, showing a gleamingly polished shine. Behind his desk was a bookshelf full of legal books and nautical decor. The walls were painted hunter green, the seats were soft red leather, and in the corner stood a Tiffany lamp that added to the room's warmth. Kieran was definitely in his own element and more comfortable to talk with Bartholomew.

"Colin and I slept with Gina as well," he confirmed the inquiry of whether or not he knew the third victim. "But not at the same time," he added with an embarrassed grin. Bartholomew did not smile, although his cheeks felt like they were turning pink. He simply nodded and jotted in his notebook.

"Were you or Colin ever jealous of these women being involved with other men?" asked Bartholomew.

"Absolutely not," replied Kieran, clearly astonished by this suggestive question.

"Sergeant, you've got to understand something. When you go out to bars and nightclubs and dance halls, you need to know that everyone is free game and that everyone views you as free game. It's all just one big meat market. Even though there are a few people who are hoping to get a relationship out of the socializing, it is an unsaid fact that everyone partying is available and wanting to get lucky at the same time. One may hope to snatch up a boyfriend or girlfriend out of it, but we all know not to expect it. Colin and I are just two carefree individuals who do not want a girlfriend, and so that scene is our scene. It's a cheap and easy hookup, and we don't expect girls to get the wrong idea about us. So, yeah, we also slept with all three of the murder victims. Does that make us look bad? Morally, yes, but you've got a lot of other men who also slept with all three of those women at some point in time. It just so happens that Colin and I were responsible enough to approach you guys and let you know our story ahead of time."

"Why did you let us know ahead of time?" asked Bartholomew.

"We thought that it would help to find their killer if we let you know a little bit about who the victims were during their lives and how we were involved with them. Plus, we were saving our own skin. If we were ever targeted as suspects, then we wanted to clear ourselves immediately before that became a possibility."

Bartholomew nodded and said, "Wow, that's commendable."

"Thank you," said Kieran.

"As long as you really meant to help us solve these crimes instead of purposely covering up your own actions by shifting suspicion away from you and Colin." Bartholomew gave Kieran a knowing smile.

"I know it can look that way also, but either way you look at it, all Colin and I can do is to show our cards faceup and hope for the best."

"I appreciate that," said Bartholomew. He continued to write in his notebook. A soft chime interrupted him. Bartholomew looked at his phone and saw that he had a text message from Lieutenant Nandyala.

"Question for you," said Bartholomew, looking at the text. "Do you know a Gloria?"

"Gloria?" Kieran said aloud. He pursed his lips and closed his eyes. "No," he said, "can't say that I do. I mean, I might, but the name doesn't ring a bell."

"How about Colin?" asked Bartholomew. "Would he know?"

"Hang on, let me ask." Kieran picked up his office phone and dialed. After a pause, he said, "Hey, Colin? Yeah, it's me. Listen, I've got Sergeant Lee here with me. He's just asking a few more questions about the murders. Hey, do you know a Gloria or about someone named Gloria?" A longer pause ensued before he got his answer and shook his head to Bartholomew. "He said he doesn't remember any Gloria. Huh?" His attention returned to what Colin was saying on the phone. It was obvious that Colin was curious about this question. Kieran said, "I'll ask. Sergeant, who is she? Someone connected to the case?"

"I am not sure," said Bartholomew. "Is there anything else that you can remember to shed light on this?"

Kieran said no and after listening to the voice on the phone, told him that Colin also said that he didn't have anything else to add.

Bartholomew thanked them and left the building of Johnson's Law Offices.

Chapter 20

Kieran was busy working away at his desk when a knock at his office door made him lift his head. It was Colin, and he looked confused.

"Are you busy with anything at the moment?" he asked Kieran.

"Not especially. Why, what's up?" Kieran put down his pen and folded his hands. Colin walked in and slumped into the chair opposite Kieran's desk.

"What do you think that was all about?" Colin asked.

"Oh, don't get the wind up, Colin," said Kieran. "They're just making routine inquiries, covering all bases, you know."

"Yeah, but what about this Gloria? Who's she?"

"How should I know?" answered Kieran. "At least I can't recall the name right now. Maybe I'll remember her later. She could have been just one of the women whom we bump into at night. She could have been one of those desperate wallflowers who get noticed by no one except for drunken men around the time that 'last call' is shouted out around the bar."

"That's a bit harsh, don't you think?" asked Colin.

"It's the harsh truth of the matter," said Kieran matter-of-factly.

Colin thought for a moment, concentrating on the matter of the murders.

"If we were to get serious about the killings," he said, "I would say that there's something odd going on with Temecula's social night life. What if the killer is some crazed maniac who loves to kill women at random? One would have to be extremely cautious in such matters. I mean we go out a lot and to a lot of places. Plus, we allow ourselves to be put into wild positions, literally speaking, and in actuality, it could be dangerous for us. Oh, I know it may not seem that way to you. I can tell by the funny way you're looking at me. I understand that it's only women who are being killed, but what if we were to stumble out of a bar one of these nights in a drunken stupor and accidently witness a murder in progress. Well, then the killer would have no choice but to murder us as well, right, rather than have any possible witnesses around? Plus, I wonder who this Gloria is. Could she be a witness herself? Could she be the killer? Sergeant Lee didn't say."

"Colin, you're overthinking this entire thing. I really don't think that we're in any danger of being stabbed anytime soon," said Kieran.

"It could happen," said Colin.

"Yes, but anything could happen," said Kieran. "You or I could get in a car accident on our way home and be dead by tonight. We can't just walk on eggshells thinking that something bad is going to happen to us around the next corner."

"I know, but until this killer is caught, we really ought to watch out for ourselves when we're out and about on the weekends."

"Tell you what," Kieran said, "I'll enjoy my drinking, and you can stay sober and keep an eye out for anyone who might look suspicious."

"Oh yes, sounds like a wonderful time for me," said Colin sarcastically. The two men laughed, and Colin left Kieran's office to return to his work.

Kieran thought about their conversation, especially the part about the woman named Gloria. He racked his brain wondering who she was. He must know her from somewhere, he thought. The name wasn't too common nowadays, so if he did know someone by that name, he would have remembered, right? But the truth of the matter was that he didn't know any Gloria. *Then why are the police so worried about her?* She must be important since the detective mentioned her, but why be so secretive about her? *Hmm ... Gloria.* Kieran decided to shake off the thought and get back to finish his work. He had a lot of paperwork that needed to be filled out, and he wanted to get it all finished before the end of the day.

Chapter 21

It was late in the evening. The air outside was much cooler at night as the season had made a definite mark upon the land, manipulating the weather to turn the temperature down, the leaves crisper, and the air to smell like fall. Nestled in the game room of the Serowik mansion were Calista, Connor, Jason Thompson, and Erin Carney. The room was warm and cozy. Connor and Jason were busy playing a game of pool while Calista and Erin had sat down to enjoy a bottle of wine and a game of chess. The boys were sipping scotch whiskey from tumblers filled with ice cubes. Connor had a bowl of chocolates close by since he always had chocolate with his scotch. He would pop one in his mouth and enjoy its melting sweetness paired with the strong taste of liquor. All four individuals seemed deeply engrossed in concentration that the sound of clicking balls was the only sound in the room. Finally, Calista spoke.

"So who do you think is killing all these women?" she asked.

"Don't know," replied Erin. She didn't look very concerned as she took a sip of her wine. "Probably some maniac who gets his jollies out of stabbing beautiful women. I wonder if he takes some item from each of his victims as a souvenir."

Calista said, "It seems odd, doesn't it, that all three women are connected to this house?"

"Not really," Jason said. "I think it's only an unfortunate coincidence. They were only short-term employees to a party your mom is putting on. The real reason for their deaths has to be connected to the party-planning business itself."

"But why start killing now? And why them?" asked Erin.

Connor hit the cue ball toward a stripe ball, and it rolled into the pocket. He said, "Maybe our house is haunted, and it's the ghosts in the walls that sensed the evil that lurked within those women, so they decided to rid the world of such wicked creatures!"

"Oh yes, I quite agree," said Calista, amused.

Connor said, "Wait a moment." He walked over to a large antique chest that was used to store board games. Connor took out boxes of board games until he finally found what he was looking for. He extracted one box from the bottom of the chest and held it out for the others to see. Calista caught her breath as she read the one word written on the box. *Ouija*.

"Oh no," she said to her brother. "You are not going to play that."

"Come on, Cali Girl," begged Connor. "We can summon the spirits of the dead girls and figure out who is committing these murders. If you think about it, we'll be helping the police."

"Ouija boards are evil and dangerous," said Erin. "Aren't there other ways we can summon the spirits?"

"We could have a séance," said Jason. He was clearly intrigued to join Connor's idea.

"We couldn't have anything of the kind," said Calista. "Besides, it's no good without a personal item from the deceased spirit to help us connect to the other side."

"Joyce, Clara, and Gina had been here, haven't they?" Jason asked. "Do you have anything of theirs that they left accidentally, even if it's a pencil or just something they touched around here?"

Calista said, "I don't believe so. And I don't know what exactly they touched around here."

Erin said, "Well, then that's that. I guess we can't play that game."

Jason and Connor groaned in disappointment, and the girls went back to their game of chess. Then suddenly, Connor snapped his fingers.

"Aha!" he cried out. "I believe I do have something that belonged to Gina!" He ran out of the game room, and in a few minutes, he returned with a black bra. Connor held it up for the rest to see. Jason raised his eyebrows while the two girls' jaws dropped in disbelief.

Calista said with horror in her voice, "Oh no, no, no, no, no! You did *not* just bring in a piece of underwear that belonged to Gina."

"Is that made out of leather?" Jason asked.

Connor continued to hold the bra high as he grinned proudly. "Yeah, she said it was expensive. I told her that I'd keep it as a ransom so as to ensure her return to rescue it. Of course, she had to pay the price to get it back."

"Don't!" called out Calista. "First of all, where did you get that from just now?"

"My room, of course," said Connor.

Calista said, "Oh my." It was obvious how Connor obtained the bra.

"Second of all," Calista said, "why keep a bra? Why couldn't you have kept a scarf or her lipstick as a memento? I can't believe you have some woman's lingerie in your room. More importantly, why do you have some *murdered* woman's lingerie in your room? The police should have been given this."

Connor protested, "And lose the only item that would remind me of Gina? Come on, Cali Girl. You know how crazy I can get over a redhead!" His mischievous eyes were gleaming.

Erin said, "That's disgusting! You should be ashamed of yourself, Connor."

"Gina was all for it," said Connor. "Come on, at least it's something to use. Where's your sense of spiritualistic adventure."

Connor called them over to the small round poker table. After he grabbed the box containing the Ouija board, he placed it in the middle of the green felt that covered the table. He folded the bra and placed it beside the board. His eyes pleaded with Calista for her cooperation, and letting out her own reluctant groan, she agreed to partake in this little ceremony of spirit summoning.

Connor said, "Calista, can you go get a candle please." Calista got up and left the room. A minute later, she returned with a single candle in its holder. Connor had already opened the box and had arranged the Ouija board in the middle of everyone. Connor lit the candle with a match and turned out the electric lights. He closed the door to the game room so as to not allow any outside light to get in. Calista closed the curtains of the windows looking outside the house. They each took a seat around the table and waited to begin. The room already seemed frightening. Setting the candle down, Connor instructed everyone to place a finger on the little piece of wood, known as the planchette. Erin, Connor, Jason, and Calista, their fingers all rested on the planchette, were now ready to ask the Ouija board their questions.

"If there is any spirit present here tonight, let us know you are here," greeted Connor. The planchette moved toward the word *Hello*. Erin started a little, but did not move her finger.

"Is the house we are now in haunted?" he asked. The planchette moved toward the word *No*.

"Well, that's a relief," said Calista sarcastically. She thought this experience was starting out to be entertaining since it clearly had to be her crazy brother manipulating the planchette.

"Ask it if it knows who the killer is," said Erin.

As if on cue, the planchette moved toward the word *Yes*. Calista and Jason both shuddered at the same time. They looked at each other with fright in their eyes and knew what the other was thinking.

"I don't know if this is such a good idea," said Jason, his voice quavering. "Maybe we should stop."

"Shh," said Connor. Then to the board, he said, "There have been three murders that happened recently around here. Three young and beautiful women were viciously stabbed to death. Do you know the ones I'm talking about?"

The board answered "Yes" to his question. Calista felt that what they were doing was ominous. Even though she didn't want to believe in ghosts, she did believe in evil spirits, and playing with an Ouija board in the dark could possibly open a portal for those evil spirits to pass through. She glanced at the candle. The little flame flickered, causing shadows to dance around them, giving the room a more frightening ambience. She looked at the other three. All of them seemed to fully understand that fact, but there seemed to be this powerful force that curiosity had impressed upon them. Although they all felt that they wanted to, none of them had removed their fingers just yet.

"Do you know who the murderer is?" asked Connor. Another answer of "Yes" followed.

"Who is the murderer?" he asked. The four young friends held their breaths, waiting for the planchette to begin moving. It did not, for a few moments, budge, but then the planchette began to move quickly. Their fingers had been thrown all around the board, one letter after the other. It was difficult to pay attention to all the letters that were spelled out, but Calista made sure to keep up. She could not believe the answer she had understood the board to spell out: "Beware of those close to you." Calista repeated the words to the others.

"What is that supposed to mean?" asked Erin. Her voice was shrill. She did not want to continue with this madness.

"It means," said Connor to Erin, "that you need to be very careful. There is a man here who has some disreputable desires upon you, and you need to lock your bedroom door tonight!" Even in the candlelight, it was evident that Jason's face had turned bright red.

"Connor!" scolded Calista. "This is serious. You don't want to make jokes in front of a Ouija board!"

Connor apologized, and they resumed their attention toward the board. Connor asked, "Can you tell us the murderer's name?" The answer this time was a firm "No." Then before they could ask it any more questions, the planchette went to the word *Goodbye* and stopped moving. The four of them removed their fingers from the heart-shaped piece and sat back in their chairs. The time it took to play with the Ouija board was only a few minutes, but the effect it had upon them would last for a while, especially in their dreams. They remained silent while they sat for a few more minutes before Connor got up and turned the lights back on in the room. Calista, Jason, and Erin sat looking at one another with wide-eyed nervousness written all over each face.

"That. Was. An. Intense. Experience," said Connor, emphasizing each word as he came back to the table. He tried to lighten the mood in the room.

"That was horrible!" exclaimed Erin.

"I second that," said Jason. "That was a bit too demonic for my taste."

"Oh, come on," said Connor. "It's just a silly game. It wasn't like it threatened us. If anything, it warned us against danger."

"Warned us? If it was really concerned about our safety, it would tell us the identity of the real killer," said Calista.

"I suppose it's against the rules of the spirit world to reveal all secrets sought from our world," said Jason thoughtfully. Then he added, "I think I need a shot of something strong before I go to bed tonight."

"Well, whatever the reason is, we still don't know who the killer is, and we should have never played with that board in the first place," said Erin.

"At least we can sleep better knowing that the Serowik Mansion is not haunted." Connor laughed.

Calista gave her brother's arm a light punch. Connor could be such a brat at times. They packed up the Ouija board and returned to their previous games. It was Jason's turn at pool, and he smacked the cue ball toward a solid ball while Connor looked on. He popped another piece of chocolate in his mouth and sipped the remaining contents of his drink. The girls took their places on either side of the chessboard, clinked their wine glasses together, sipped, and finished their game. The evening started out uneventful, but after their experience with the Ouija board, it was almost certain that none of them would get much sleep that night.

There was one thing still that continued to gnaw at Calista's mind. Why did her brother have an item, a piece of lingerie from one of the victims? *When did the two of them have sex?* she wondered. And most importantly, why didn't he inform the detectives of his relationship with her? Could he have slept with the other two victims as well? Her mind wandered for a terrible moment, imagining an idea that her brother could have developed a killer's taste for blood. Calista immediately scratched that out of her mind. How could she think of such a thing about her brother? Then again, he was the wild child out of the two of them. But no, *absolutely not.* This was going way too far. The mood of this evening was causing her to think up some disturbing concepts. More than likely, she was feeling the effects that the Ouija board experience had impressed upon her mind. However, she did spend the rest of the night letting her mind occasionally wander toward thoughts about these questions, and most importantly, Calista wondered what she should do about it.

Chapter 22

Margaret was humming along to the music blasting from the speakers in her car. She had just come home from getting her hair done. *There's nothing like a good color and style to brighten up one's day,* she thought. She drove her silver Jaguar into the garage and was about to close the garage door when she heard a male voice call to her. She stopped and turned to see Cirenio, their landscaper, jog up to her. Panting a little, he leaned forward and took a moment to slow down his breathing.

"Mrs. Serowik," he said, "I have something to tell you that may seem very important."

"Yes, Cirenio?" said Margaret, suddenly feeling excited from his energy. "What is it? Is everything all right?"

"Yes. Do you remember when I suggested that my wife, Christine, help out with your party?" he began.

"Of course, she was here when Joyce and I were going over the particulars. Such a pretty little thing your wife is, so darling and petite."

"Well, that night at the dinner table, she told me some pretty revealing things. She said that Joyce Galway was a horrible person and should never be trusted. In fact, Christine was thinking about staying by my side the entire time Joyce would be here so as to keep her from noticing me and sinking her claws into the gardener. She said that Joyce has the reputation of being a, well, a ..."

"It's okay, Cirenio. I'm finding out more and more that she was indeed a slut," finished Margaret. Then she huffed and said, "I don't really care about anyone's personal love life. What people do in the privacy of their homes is none of my business, but when people whom I've hired to do a job get bumped off because of something they did in their personal lives, well then, that's just horribly rude and a damned nuisance for me. Why couldn't those girls get murdered some other time, instead of having it done during the preparations for my Halloween party? Any other time of the year would be much more convenient for all of us."

"Um, yes, ma'am. Anyway, like I was saying, Christine said that it didn't matter who Joyce could grab as far as men were concerned. Apparently, Joyce likes to broaden her horizon of conquests from rich entrepreneurs to trash picker-uppers. According to my wife, Joyce's type is all types—single or taken. All that mattered was her own sexual needs."

"Well, at least I can take comfort in knowing that she didn't try to seduce my husband," said Margaret, relieved. But then she said, "Wait a minute. Maybe she doesn't find Richard good enough to include in her types. Well, that's definitely rude of her. If you think about it, I should take offense."

"Offense because she didn't try to hit on your husband, ma'am?" Cirenio knew Mrs. Serowik was a quirky rich lady, and he was used to it, but this was downright funny.

"Of course! Wouldn't you be offended if a good-looking man found every other woman attractive but ignored your wife? But that's getting off the point. Tell me, how does your wife know Joyce?"

"She went to school with her back in the day," answered Cirenio. "My wife saw a lot of bad things that Joyce did, pretty cruel things that my wife felt could be perceived as inhumane. From what she told me, Joyce seemed like a real witch."

"Well, the more I'm learning about Joyce, I'd have to agree. Your poor wife, she was probably scared of Joyce," said Margaret.

"Sort of, but the real reason why Christine knows her so well is because she was one of the Bully Bohos, and she was right alongside Joyce and their other friends being mean and spiteful around the school."

Margaret nodded, understanding Cirenio's need to call her attention to this. There had been three too many murders happening, and maybe Cirenio's wife could shed some light on the case. In any event, she figured that they needed to talk to Lieutenant Ram Nandyala and Sergeant Bartholomew Lee as soon as possible.

"Why don't we all gather here in the house with the detectives and have your wife tell them all about her past with the victims," suggested Margaret.

Cirenio agreed.

"Can you contact your wife and have her meet us here?" asked Margaret.

Cirenio said, "Of course." He took his phone out of his back pocket, slid his thumb across the face of it to open, and tapped on his wife's name in the favorites section of the contacts. While he was talking to her, Margaret opened her purse, took out her phone and the business card containing Lieutenant Ram Nandyala's number. She dialed the number printed on the card and spoke to Ram.

Forty minutes later, the Serowik mansion's living room included the following people: Lieutenant Ram Nandyala, Sergeant Bartholomew Lee, Margaret Serowik, and Cirenio and Christine Ulster. Connie had been in and had just finished serving tea. She then left, closing the doors to the room behind her to give the occupants privacy.

Ram stood next to the fireplace while he held his cup and saucer in front of him. He looked down at the small figure of a woman who seemed nervous to be there. *Such a tiny woman,* he thought, *even smaller than Calista, who is already a petite woman.* Being a tall man with long arms and legs and big feet, Ram had to shop for clothing specific to his size. He couldn't shop at the big and tall section since he wasn't a big man. He was quite lean. And he couldn't shop at the average-sized men's section because of his height. He wondered if the woman sitting before him also had that issue when she went clothes shopping. He imagined that she would probably have to shop in the junior's section of clothing departments, which didn't provide much of a style fit for her age. It was a bit difficult when some people had to shop in departments that don't seem to match their age group.

Christine Ulster looked nervous as she sat on the antique sofa alongside her husband, who held her hand in a comforting manner.

Ram took a sip of his tea, still hot, replaced the white cup, which had a border of leaves delicately painted in gold, and began.

"Mrs. Ulster," Ram said, "may I call you Christine?" Ram wanted the woman to feel comfortable. His warm demeanor had put the woman he addressed at ease. She nodded her consent. From her seat, Christine thought that he acted as though he could be her older brother, so reassuring and understanding. He had the kind of disposition that could make anyone confess to anything.

"Thank you. Christine, it has come to my understanding that you not only knew the first victim of the stabbings that occurred recently, but that you knew her personally. She was a friend, perhaps, at one time?"

Christine looked up from her seat and said after clearing her throat, "I knew all three of the girls stabbed."

The gasp from Margaret was the only sound heard after Christine's statement. Ram nodded for her to continue.

Christine took a sip from her own cup, cleared her throat a second time, sat up straight, and said, "First, you need to know that I was a different person back then, as a child, I mean. I am also ashamed to be here today in front of you, but I also realize that there have been three deaths, and if there is any way I can prevent another from occurring, I am here to tell you what I know about the whole thing." The whole room was quiet as they listened.

Christine coughed. "Anyway, I'll start out with a little bit of my own background. It may be important or not, but, well, here goes. I was an Army brat, so I had been to a few different schools before my dad retired and settled here. It's a normal thing for most military families to move after a short period of time in one town, and we moved a lot. I was going into fifth grade when my family moved here in Temecula, and I knew nobody. It's not any fun moving, especially when you establish close relationships with friends and then have to lose them. But the good thing about not knowing anyone in the new town is that you can reinvent yourself and make yourself whomever you want to be. And by fifth grade, I wanted to be popular with popular friends. That was really important to me since I never had enough time to become well-known at my previous schools. So here,

I told everyone who would listen that I had been the cheerleading captain on a cheerleading squad in my previous hometown. I told everyone that I had a boyfriend and that he missed me so much. I even showed pictures of my older cousin, who was really cute, and told everyone that he was my boyfriend. Soon, and I don't know how or when it came about, Joyce and Clara approached me and asked if I wanted to hang out with them. They told me that they were part of an exclusive clique, and they called themselves the Bohos Beauties. The name Boho Bullies came later when people had the nerve to call them that. Anyway, they asked me to join them, and I couldn't have said yes quick enough. For me, it was exhilarating. It didn't matter that I was the new girl. I was a popular girl, had friends who respected me, and I had made a mark for myself in school by simply fabricating a bunch of stuff.

"Gina was also part of the group, as well as a few other girls, but it was a pretty close-knit group. There were others in the past, but they had fallen out with Joyce and were no longer part of the group. Joyce Galway was definitely the leader—there was no doubt about that. There was some kind of *I'm in charge* attitude about her, and we all followed suit. I think that we all didn't really know what we were supposed to do in our group of popular girls, and it was nice to have someone think up some activities for us to do, how we were supposed to act, and how we should dress as a group with good fashion sense.

"It only took a little while for me to really see the bullying. But even though Joyce started the bullying, we all joined in, partly for fear of losing our credibility with her and partly because we enjoyed hurting others. I'm ashamed to admit this, but it made us feel powerful. And the things we did were brutal. There was this one time when Joyce told us to spread a rumor that our seventh-grade math teacher, Mr. Ellis, was having an affair with the English teacher, Mrs. Smith. Of course, not a shred of it was true even though their classrooms were close to each other and the two teachers could be seen exchanging friendly words with each other. We were so good about making that rumor stick that both their marriages broke up, and Mr. Ellis had moved to a different city. Want to know the even more disgusting truth of the entire matter? The motive that had lain behind all that was the fact that Joyce was failing math, and it looked like she was going to be forced to attend summer school. Therefore, she felt that Mr. Ellis had to be punished for issuing her grade. Mrs. Smith was simply an innocent bystander that Joyce used to complete her mission. Well, actually, she wasn't just a random bystander. Mrs. Smith was actually good-looking—sexy, in fact—and all the junior high school boys loved to fantasize about her. And that was not going to fly for Joyce, who felt that every straight male should be fantasizing about no one else but her.

"Anyway, after that whole ordeal, Joyce was never called out on what she did. Everyone pretty much knew what she did, but there wasn't any concrete proof of her actions, and it seemed like no one had the guts to confront her on it. And that was only one instance concerning teachers. There were others' lives that suffered from Joyce's methods of ruin. Actually, I should say all of our methods of ruin since we all were active participants. I just say Joyce, since she was the driving force behind our mischief."

Christine took a deep breath and continued, "As far as the students were concerned, Joyce would insult, berate, and spread even more viciously cruel rumors. If some girl pissed her off or even did something as simple as look at her funny, Joyce had us help her spread rumors of that particular girl having a sexually transmitted disease or something equally horrible. She spread lies about some students' parents being drug addicts, abusers, molesters, etc. Joyce was also tall and beautiful, and encouraged all of us to have our hair, face, and nails perfectly done as if we were ready for a daily photo shoot. So it wasn't any wonder that we all got any guy we wanted. That would have been fine, except for the fact that Joyce took it too far. If she wanted some girl's boyfriend, she would simply take him. She'd just walk up to him and start to flirt shamelessly no matter who was watching. Sometimes she would flirt right in front of the girlfriend. And boys that age were no match for Joyce. They couldn't resist her charm. It seemed that boys also wanted her approval as well as us girls.

"I finally had enough of those bullies, or Boho Beauties, I should say, when an incident occurred. It was during this time when we all saw that Joyce's torment had taken a tragic turn. There was this girl, I forget what her name was, but she was a fellow student. The girl was short, a little round, and she had bad acne. She used to be so happy-go-lucky and friendly with everyone. In fact, she helped me with my chemistry class because I just couldn't get all those chemical abbreviations and formulas. I was complaining about how difficult the class was, and she overheard me. She came over to where I sat and offered to help me with my homework. You see, she was really smart and didn't bat an eyeball about helping me. She didn't seem to have any close friends, and I thought that she was helping me because I was one of the popular girls. Shoot! What was her name?" Christine's hand went to her forehead in an effort to remember.

"Anyway, we had only met a few times, twice after school in the park and once at the mall. Joyce caught me with that girl one day at the mall. We were eating lunch at the food court while she tutored me on an upcoming chemistry exam. Joyce blatantly made fun of her in front of anyone around who watched. She was saying how fat the girl was, how ugly she was, pointing out her acne and saying how her face looked like a pepperoni pizza. I tried to get Joyce to stop, telling her that the girl was just there helping me to prepare for an exam. But Joyce went on telling the girl that she was not worthy to even consider hanging out with anyone from her group of Bohos, especially in a public place. The girl hurried to gather her stuff, apologized to me, and quickly walked out of the mall. She apologized to me as if this was all her fault!"

Tears fell from Christine's face as she recalled this memory. Her face was now red with embarrassment, and she was hugging her body tight. The room was completely silent, save for the scratching of Sergeant Lee's pen on his notepad. Christine went on with her story.

"I didn't tell Joyce to go stick it, nor did I go after the girl to apologize. Instead, I just sat there in the cafeteria, dumbfounded. But I will tell you this. It was definitely an eye-opening moment for me. After that day, I thought that the whole thing would just be forgotten, but I was wrong. Oh, man, was I wrong. You know how someone finds that they have a talent for something, and once they get a taste of that talent, they work hard to perfect that skill of theirs?

Well, Joyce had a talent for meanness, and the more she practiced on being a mean girl, the more she enjoyed it and was never fully satisfied. She had to ruin as many lives as she could in order to feed her sick sadistic nature. It wasn't any wonder that Joyce had thoroughly enjoyed the emotional beating she executed on that girl and was not finished there. Her tongue went to work, wagging at anyone and everyone who would listen, and that was basically everyone. She told people that the girl got those spots because she had a skin disease that was contagious. You can imagine that there wasn't a single student who wanted to sit next to the girl. In fact, students treated her like she was a walking plague so much that the girl had to sit by herself in each class, at lunch, and on the bus.

"Joyce made fun of her weight so much that the girl ended up not eating at all. Instead, the girl lost a lot of weight, so much that we could see her bones sticking out of her skin. The girl just seemed to envelope herself in this cocoon, probably to keep safe, but it only made things worse. It would probably be better if she was simply forgotten, but because Joyce had this constant poisonous spotlight on her, living was horrible for the girl. The teasing never ceased, the isolated treatment continued, and one day, just like that, the girl disappeared, never to be seen or heard from again."

Ram said, "It is truly fascinating to realize that one young girl could be in possession of so much power. I hope that you do know how much I appreciate this revelation. This couldn't have been easy for you to drag through such unpleasant memories. However, it may help shed light upon the case. You must also know that I never have been nor ever will be a judgmental person. I also assure you that everything you reveal here will not leave this room as far as I am concerned." Ram looked toward Margaret.

She understood the look and said, "Of course, Lieutenant. My lips are sealed."

Ram nodded then asked, "By any chance, Christine, what grade were you in when this girl disappeared?"

Christine looked up at the ceiling then answered, "I think it was eleventh grade. Wait, yeah, because that was the year that I took chemistry. And, Detective, you must know that I am full of remorse for playing my part in the Boho Beauties' activities. My entire focus was on my image and not the feelings of others. How I wish I could go back and apologize profusely to everyone, especially to that girl."

"And the name of this girl; you cannot recall?"

Christine shook her head.

Ram took a few steps closer to her before he asked softly, "Christine, was her name Gloria?"

Christine's eyes lit up. "Yes! How could I forget? Her name was Gloria. But how on earth could you have known that?" she said.

Ram didn't answer her question but simply followed with "Do you happen to remember her last name?"

When Christine shook her head with a definite no, Ram turned, placed his cup and saucer back on the serving tray, and without an explanation to the rest of the room's occupants, left the room. Sergeant Lee looked surprised by his partner's sudden departure, but he said nothing and just followed in step behind him.

When the other three people in the living room heard the front entrance doors slam shut, Margaret, Cirenio, and Christine all looked from one to another, jaws open. No one knew what to do or say at that moment. Margaret let out a low whistle.

"Oh my," she said, "this case is getting good—really, really good." Margaret took a long sip from her cup and swallowed the tea in one loud gulp.

"Um, do any of you know why he just left so suddenly?" asked Cirenio. Margaret and Christine shook their heads, but Margaret had a feeling that Lieutenant Ram Nandyala had a very good reason for his unexpected departure.

Chapter 23

Bartholomew sat in the driver's seat quietly concentrating on the road while Ram was busy dialing contacts and talking on the phone. Bartholomew did not know why they left so abruptly. He thought that there might have been more that Christine Ulster could have shared, but Ram decided that it was more important to leave. This was just another of Ram's little odd quirks during an investigation, and though some might find his behavior impulsively rude, Bartholomew understood that there was a good reason; and if he was patient, it would all soon be revealed, putting to rest any questions he might have.

When Ram had finished his final call, he sat back in the passenger seat and let out a satisfied sigh. This confused Bartholomew; however, he said nothing. They pulled into the parking lot of the police station and walked inside. When they arrived at Ram's office, the sweet sounds of nature emanating from the speaker mixed with the delicate aroma of incense welcomed them. Bartholomew always felt as though he was walking into a spa, and could not help but become enveloped by the feeling of relaxation. Ram began to make some tea. Then he sat, folded his hands on his desk, closed his eyes, and waited. Bartholomew also sat and closed his eyes. He occasionally opened one eye to see if Ram had moved or opened his eyes, but Ram did not budge. A few minutes went by, and the water in the tea maker began to boil. Ram got up from his seat, grabbed two cups, and prepared the tea. Once he was finished, he turned and handed a cup to Bartholomew, who accepted. The two blew on their tea to cool the temperature and sipped in silence.

Bartholomew cleared his throat and said, "Sir? Are we, um, waiting on something?"

Ram lifted a palm up and said softly, "Patience, my dear Bartholomew. Patience. Drink your tea. I made it strong to energize us."

A knock on the door soon interrupted their brief time of relaxation, and the sound of it brought a smile to Ram's lips. "Ah, the time has arrived. Brace yourself, Sergeant Lee. Our short time of rest and relaxation has now come to an end. The answers I requested on the ride over here have begun to arrive, and we have much work to do."

Bartholomew smiled. He should have expected this. Ram's exterior manner might appear resigned and relaxed, but inside that head of his, the cogs and wheels were continuously running.

The officer who knocked on the door came in and handed Ram a small stack of papers stapled together. Ram showed Bartholomew the stack, which looked like a report.

Ram said, "As soon as Christine mentioned the particular girl, who we now know as Gloria, as one of the victims who was bullied in such a severe manner by Joyce and her crew of Boho Beauties, I figured that there might be a possibility that Gloria is the reason for these stabbings. For some reason, it all ties to her, and if we look at her in particular, we will soon solve the case."

"Do you think that Gloria could be our killer and that she is stabbing all these Boho Beauties as an act of revenge?" asked Bartholomew.

"It's a definite possibility, but we have to be certain. That is why I asked for a background report on any girl named Gloria who went to Everest High School from 2005 to 2008, and who also fit closely to the physical details that matched what Christine had described to us." He scanned over the report before continuing.

"And it looks like I found her," said Ram triumphantly. "Her name is Gloria Wjoinowski, and I have here her school portrait photos from freshman to her junior year of high school. It seems to be the girl whom Christine Ulster spoke about. Look here, Bartholomew. Do you see how in her freshman year, 2005 to 2006, Gloria was round, and those look like they could be the pockmarks from the acne?" He pointed to the black-and-white photo. Looking up at Bartholomew was a face of a girl who didn't smile, nor did she frown.

He tried to figure out what she was feeling during the time that photo was taken. Even though she didn't flash a toothy smile back at the camera, she didn't look like she was sad either. It was difficult to read the girl's expression.

Bartholomew took a deeper look at her. The girl in the photo wore a blank expression. Her jaw was lifted, as if she was trying to look up, but her eyes remained straight, looking toward the camera lens. He surmised that she wasn't a girl who seemed to mind or bother anyone. Bartholomew couldn't tell if Gloria was depressed during her first year of high school, but as he picked up Gloria's sophomore year's photo, he saw an obvious difference in the girl's appearance. She had lost weight—a lot, in fact—and her expression was thoroughly unhappy when that photo was taken. Her eyes were sunken and hollow, a pained expression written on the girl's face. It was easy to see that she was not at all happy.

Then he looked at Gloria's yearbook photo taken during her junior year of high school. The results were so dramatic that he had to look twice in order to somewhat recognize the image. The acne marks were still there, but the girl had dropped an extreme amount of weight compared to the year before, making her look unhealthy, small, and pathetic. Her hair was cut short, butchered in a sense, he thought, showing a wild mess of spikes. She wore a choker, and her nose was pierced. Her lips were painted with a dark shade of lipstick, and the part of her skin that didn't have acne was as white as chalk. Bartholomew's eyes seemed to pop out of his head as he stared in amazement. *Such a dramatic change,* he thought to himself. Was this really the same girl in each photo? Ram seemed to hear his thoughts.

"It's the same girl," he said, sighing.

"Dang! What a shame," said Bartholomew. "It makes me want to go back to that time, seek her out, and help her. Who's to know what kind of life she would have had if she didn't fall victim to a bitch like Joyce?" He was now wondering why they were putting in so much effort to find the killer of these horrible women who, when one thought about it, actually deserved more than a stabbing. If they really were as bad as everyone said they were, these girls deserved to be tortured within an inch of their lives. But, Bartholomew realized, that was his knee-jerk reaction, and murder was murder, no matter what the reason. No matter what one thought to be a justified killing, taking someone's life could never be excused. The killer needed to be caught and punished, especially before anyone else got killed.

He looked at Ram. "I know that it seems that this Gloria Wjoinoski is some type of clue, but we didn't come across her in this investigation. The only thing that we have is her name shouted out by one of our victims before she died. We don't even know where this Gloria Wjoinoski can be found."

Ram smiled. "And that is step two. I've already asked that once Gloria was found, a background check would be performed to find out where she went after she disappeared during her junior year of high school. I think that since her last name is not very common, it shouldn't be too difficult to find her." Another knock on the door interrupted them.

"Oh my, how I do love technology!" said Ram in a giddy sounding voice. He beckoned the officer behind the door in, who opened the door and handed Bartholomew the second set of paperwork: the file of a Ms. Gloria Wjoinoski.

"Hmm," said Ram. "It looks like Gloria was admitted into Mountainside Rehab Center after a period of drug use."

"That seems to make sense, after what I saw in those photos. Who admitted her?" asked Bartholomew.

"The police," answered Ram. "She was caught stealing at a department store and then booked because they found her to be in possession of crack cocaine. When she was arrested, the girl was five feet, five inches, ninety pounds, and addicted to drugs. When asked if she had any family, she replied that she had none, was nineteen years of age, and because they couldn't find any identification that indicated she was lying, they believed her story and enrolled her in the process of rehabilitation. She was diagnosed with anorexia nervosa, drug addiction, and social anxiety. Later, it was found out that she was lying about her age and about not having any family. They got in touch with a mother who ended up paying for the girl's rehab expenses. There doesn't seem to be any father around. There's no mention of a father's name, and it doesn't look like she had any siblings. By the time Gloria got out, a year and a half had passed. After that, there is nothing. It was as if she then disappeared from there and was never heard from again."

"They didn't take her fingerprints?" asked Bartholomew. "It would have proved helpful in finding out where she went after rehab."

"There is no mention of fingerprints taken, even at the time of her arrest. I wonder if they just dropped the charges since she was being admitted into the rehab. They were probably too concerned with her getting better," said Ram. "Also, the issues of confidentiality within the rehab center may have been a contributing factor to her anonymity. It is a delicate issue when dealing with getting people better and infringing on their personal lives."

"Do you think that there might have been some sort of DNA evidence pointing to her identity there? Even a small amount like preserved blood samples of previous patients?"

"I'm sure it doesn't hurt to ask," said Ram. "We'll need to prepare though and have a warrant at the ready. Just in case we come across some obstacle, like the rehab's protocol, of course."

"Of course," agreed Bartholomew. He looked down at the report and perused it some more. The only other important pieces of information contained notes on the medications that were prescribed to Gloria Wjoinoski during her treatment and written explanations about her reaction to those medications. There were also doctor and nurse's comments about various matters that required their professional input.

Ram picked up his office phone and began dialing a series of important numbers. It didn't take long for the detectives to learn that there was absolutely no DNA that was left at the rehab center. The rehab center did take blood and urine samples from patients when they had to test for drugs, but the contents were soon disposed of once the testing was finished. However, they were able to learn that Gloria's blood type was A positive and that she entered Mountainside on October 7, 2007, and was discharged from Mountainside on May 3, 2009. That would make her stay there to be a year and seven months. Ram asked the representative of Mountainside Rehab Center if any of the staff had been working there during that time.

When it was confirmed that there were a few employees present at that time, Ram asked to make an appointment to visit so that he could ask them some questions. The representative said that would be fine and gave Ram a few times that would be most convenient. Ram thanked her and hung up.

Bartholomew said, "So we know that a Ms. Gloria Wjoinoski exited rehab after a year and a half, and that was all anyone seemed to hear from her. But what's confusing me is that there's no way she could have simply vanished into thin air. If she had a drug problem that she was trying to tackle, then she might have had relapses and returned to some type of treatment center for help. She might have gotten a job, got married, become pregnant; or gotten something that would help us find her."

"And that is why we have much work to do," said Ram.

Bartholomew nodded. He and Ram discussed their next plan of attack, and Bartholomew exited the office and its ambience of serene comfort to begin.

Chapter 24

Fitz still had an hour to go before his shift ended. The medic engineer scheduled to be his relief had come in early, so he was able to prepare his bedding and toiletries and pack them in his truck while he waited for the shift to end. He had just finished a day of overtime at station 40 and was tired. The previous night was busy. There was an overdose at one point. It was a young girl who took a bunch of pills because her boyfriend had broken up with her. Fitz had to give her a cocktail of activated charcoal and make her drink it down. The girl had a bit of an attitude and didn't want to drink the nasty stuff, but Fitz's captain had spoken sternly to her saying that she had done this to herself and that if she wanted to continue to live without fully messing up her insides, then she needed to get the pills out of her system. Fitz marveled at the stupidity some people had. Attempting to kill oneself over love was the silliest action, he thought, but unfortunately, it was a part of life. However, it didn't help that Fitz and the rest of the crew had to leave their nice warm beds in order to tend to a stupid person like this girl. But that was part of the job, and even though that was one of the negative aspects of being a paramedic, he did love his chosen profession. Even though it was hard work, Fitz felt this sense of accomplishment after each shift. He also couldn't wait to get home to his little apartment, take a much-deserved long, hot shower, and relax by playing a few hours on his computer game, Danger Quest.

"Every firefighter," Fitz's training officer had stressed to his class while he was in the academy, "needs something enjoyable to do after every shift." His training officer explained that the reason for this was to embrace one's own means of relaxation, whether it was putting together puzzles, reading books, or working on model airplanes.

That statement was followed with laughter throughout the classroom. It didn't take Fitz long to figure out what activity he enjoyed doing during his downtime. He was never a reader, and he didn't like to spend hours at the gym when he got home. He also didn't have any hobbies, nor did he like to hang out with his buddies at the bar. He didn't really like alcohol, save for the occasional single beer or glass of wine at dinner. No, Fitz was the type of person who was more of a homebody. He loved visiting his parents, who lived just thirty minutes away from his apartment, in a town called Romoland. Anytime he visited them, he was welcomed with the delicious aromas of a meal on the stove and a dessert in the oven. His father, always one who seemed forever glued to his favorite chair in the living room, would holler out a hello toward Fitz and a beckoning gesture with his arm to sit on one of the sofas and join him while he watched the latest sports game on television. His mother, prompted by the loud booming voice of his father, would rush toward the sounds of male conversation and wrap her large soft arms around her son. Then his mother would make him sit back on the sofa and talk with his father while she checked on her cooking. He loved his parents, and he loved visiting the home he had grown up in. His parents had kept the house clean and homey, so much so that a perfect stranger would immediately feel comfortable, as if one were part of the family.

Fitz slid the electronic key into his apartment and let himself in. As soon as he was inside, he dropped the large duffel bag that had contained his personal necessary items that he used when he worked overtime at a station different from his home station. After a shower, a shave, and a meal of chicken nuggets and peas—all products from his freezer, cooked quickly in his microwave—Fitz was about to settle in for an evening of Danger Quest when he suddenly didn't want to play. Instead, his mind had wandered and had stuck on one subject: Calista Serowik. She was such a pretty girl, friendly and upbeat. She seemed to enjoy their date together the other night. In fact, when he asked if he could call her again, she had said, "Yes, that would be great." He looked at his watch. It was ten o'clock in the morning. Did she just get off work also? He decided to take a chance to call her. Anyway, if she wasn't free to talk, he could simply leave her a message.

The cell phone rang three times before he heard a "Hey there, Fitz."

"Hi, Calista. Sorry to bother you," he said.

"No, in fact, I was just rifling through some girly magazine. So your call came at the perfect moment," Calista said, giggling a little.

"I, um, was calling to ask if …" *Damn,* he thought. He suddenly felt so nervous that his throat suddenly felt dry. He cleared it as best he could before continuing.

"I was calling to see if you would like to grab dinner tonight?" he managed to say.

There was a momentary pause. Was she actually contemplating saying no? Probably.

On the other end of the line, Calista was thinking about this evening and whether or not it would be a good idea to go out, especially since the killer of these stabbings was still at large. Her parents had suggested that she stay inside the mansion for a while for her own safety, but it wouldn't be like she was alone tonight; and she wasn't planning on going to a club or a bar. She was just going out to dinner, so it shouldn't be dangerous for her.

"I would love to go to dinner with you," she said finally. She didn't hear the exhalation of relief from Fitz's end of the call.

"We could meet up at Bo's Burgers for a hamburger," she said. "It's pretty easy to find because it's like right next to the hospital."

"Whoa! Slow down there, Nursie!" Fitz said laughing.

"Oh, yeah, sorry, Fitz. I'm game for anything really," Calista went on. "Tacos, sushi, spaghetti, steak, chicken, vegetarian? I like all food, so it's your choice."

Fitz's laughter now bellowed out in boisterous joviality. When he calmed down, he said through giggles, "I, ah, was kind of hoping to take you out to a nice restaurant, maybe wine and dine you for a bit. Let me charm you for a little bit before we move on to grabbing burgers?" Calista could imagine seeing his smiling eyes on the other end of the connection and couldn't help but be moved by his romantic idea.

"Of course," she said. "Don't mind me. It's just that I ramble on when I'm nervous. It's okay, you can go ahead and charm me." Calista took a deep audible breath.

Fitz would have laughed some more at her evident awkwardness, but he was busy thinking about her admission of being nervous. She really was too cute. He found it flattering, especially since he was concerned before that maybe she wasn't as attracted to him as he was to her. That was always the problem when one dated someone in particular. There's this expectation of being oneself without showing one's bad side, while at the same time studying the other person so as to decipher later whether or not this was a good match. After the initial attraction, people had to evaluate the other person's character, beliefs and disbeliefs, daily practice of living, and whether or not that person is worthy to introduce to one's own mother. At least in Fitz's case, that latter trait was the most important. His mother would kill him if he introduced her to a girl who didn't meet her standards. His mother was kind and loving, and he could always count on leaving her house with a satisfied, bursting belly whenever he visited his parents.

Fitz suggested a local Italian restaurant. It was a mom-and-pop type of place, and it held the balanced quality of being informal and elegant at the same time. By the time they arrived, the lights were dimmed, and each table included a lit candle and a single white rose sitting on top of a deep burgundy–colored tablecloth. The waiter brought them breadsticks and took their order. Fitz ordered a bottle of merlot, and the waiter sprinted off to get their wine. Calista was wearing a simple but stunning emerald-green strapless dress that complimented her eyes and her midnight-colored hair, half of it pulled up and pinned in perfectly coifed curls. The hairstyle allowed any onlooker to view her slender neck, bare except for a single black-strapped choker. She wore black heels, which made her feel more of an average-height woman in contrast to the reality of her normally short self. From where Fitz was sitting, he remembered how he had been immediately attracted to her good looks and friendly nature. However, tonight, in the midst of flickering candles emanating from each of the tables, causing shadows to dance methodically around the restaurant walls, Calista was a vision of absolute perfection.

"You look so stunningly beautiful," said Fitz for what seemed like the fifth time since picking her up from her home.

Calista giggled and blushed behind her menu. "You look very handsome as well," she said.

"Why thank you, Nursie." He reached across the small table to hold her hand.

"Oh, before I forget, my mother asked if you'd please come to the party. I'm sorry it's not a formal invitation, but this year is proving to be a bit unconventional in comparison to the years past," said Calista.

"I think that would be fun," said Fitz. "As long as I don't get murdered, of course." His face twisted in an odd grin. "Too soon?" he asked.

Calista smiled. "I don't think so. One of the things they teach us in nursing school is to laugh at tragedy. Not in a scoffing or teasing sort of way against those who suffer from the tragedy, but in a way that will help us detach from any emotional connection to the tragedy. This way, we can focus better on keeping our heads clear and our patients safe."

Fitz said, "I know. We're taught the same thing in paramedic school, and believe me, we practice it a lot. There's nothing like a horrible traffic collision involving people who remind you of someone you know, catching you off guard and ruining your ability to apply your best performance."

They paused a moment in their conversation when the waiter came back with their wine. He poured the wine in each of their glasses, and after setting the bottle down, he took their order. Once they gave the waiter their order, Fitz and Calista picked up their wine glasses and toasted to each other. They sipped their wine, and Calista thought it was a full-bodied blend that was quite good. Then they settled into more serious conversation.

Calista said, "So what do you think about these local murders? There've been three so far, and maybe there might be more. My mother is in an absolutely fretful state."

"I can imagine," agreed Fitz. "It is a pretty scary thing being a female around town right now, unless the killer decides to shift genders in his victims."

"No, you don't understand. You'd think that taking precautions as a female is her first priority, but not my mother. Instead, she's in a fretful state over the fact that her party might be canceled this year!"

"Seriously? Even though her life could have been in danger, and may still be in danger? And what about you? You really need to be extremely careful as well."

"I know. I almost said no to this date tonight," admitted Calista. "But then I realized that it would be all right as long as I was with you."

Fitz beamed at this comment, but then he asked, "Is it really true that all three murders are related to your family in some way?"

"Actually, yes and no. Isn't that weird? I mean, it's not like we have an intimate connection to them, but all three were contracted by my mother to plan and coordinate this party. You see, every year, my mother puts on these spectacular Halloween parties. It's her favorite holiday of the year, and my parents can afford the lavish luxury." Calista blushed for a moment, because her mother always taught her that bragging about their family's money was always an act of poor taste. She continued.

"She hires an event coordinator in order to plan every detail. To begin with, there are tables full of appetizers and an open bar available. This helps to put everyone at ease while introductions are made and social niceties are gotten out of the way. Once everyone has settled in with drinks and small bites to eat, a more structured part of the evening commences. Dinner is served in the formal dining room. Once everyone has finished, they are then ushered to the living room where they all play three or four competitive games refereed by my mother and with prizes to win. Then when the party is over, everyone can do whatever they please. They can continue to drink the night away. They can retreat to the library for some quiet reading. We also provide decks of cards and board games in the living room for those who want to play. Clue was always the most popular game during the parties in the past. If some guests are tired, they can retreat to their rooms to relax. We have twenty rooms, and while the party is going on, the servants are busy taking all the overnight bags to each guest's assigned room. This is a huge convenience for those who really want to enjoy the full effects of the evening. The next day, breakfast is served along with coffee and aspirin for those who have hangovers, and everyone goes home. It's a lot of fun. Well, this year, Mother decided to change up her annual party by hosting a murder mystery theme. I, of course, was excited since I love to curl up with a good mystery; and to experience an old-fashioned murder mystery in person? Well, that would be just too thrilling!"

Fitz said, "But how do the murder victims come into it?"

"I'm getting to that," said Calista, then continued, "So my mother hired an event coordinator recommended to her, and she knew how to put on a murder mystery show. That was Joyce, and the other two girls killed were hired by Joyce to work that evening. It turns out they all knew each other from way, way back in elementary school. But to top that off, they all frequented the same kind of places, like bars and dance clubs, and they slept with the majority of Temecula's male population."

"They didn't sleep with me," said Fitz. "But I'm not really a partygoer myself. I've been to some social hangouts, but that was a guy's night out with some buddies of mine. But I'm sure they wouldn't even notice me."

"I don't see why not," protested Calista. "You're very good looking, and you can hold a conversation as well as listen attentively."

"Thanks," said Fitz, "but guys my height don't get that much attention, especially from tall girls. I could have the prettiest face in the world, but without height, I might as well be an average Joe."

"Hmm, I suppose that you have something there," agreed Calista. "Although I wouldn't know what being a tall girl would be like. Everyone, to me, is tall, including midgets."

"That's funny, Nursie," Fitz said. He lifted his glass.

"To short people," he said.

"To short people," she repeated, and their glasses clinked.

Their food arrived and the two ate. They conversed sparingly in between bites, about their likes and dislikes, what they did during their days off, and other small details about themselves.

By the time Fitz had dropped her off at her front door and declined an invitation to come in, he gently kissed Calista on the cheek and asked her if he could call her sometime soon. Calista eagerly agreed, and the two parted ways; she through the front door of her parents' home, and he down the long driveway.

Chapter 25

The next afternoon, Dr. Neville Williams caught Calista at her station, busy filling out reports and humming to herself.

"Hi, Calista," he said.

"Oh, hi, Neville," said Calista, looking up from her work. "How've you been doing?" She smiled at him.

Neville coughed and said unconvincingly, "Great. Um, I wanted to come by earlier to talk to you about something. When you go to lunch, can you come and get me, and I'll treat us at the cafeteria?"

"Sure." She narrowed her eyes humorously and said with a hint of tease in her voice, "Sounds kind of mysterious."

Neville said, "It's not, really, but there's a few things I'd like to go over with you privately, and that's pretty much the only place and time where we can accomplish that."

Calista agreed, and Neville left.

When her lunchtime came, Calista sought out Dr. Williams, which didn't take long since he was in his office. They walked down to the cafeteria exchanging pleasantries about what was new in their lives. Dr. Williams chose a chicken salad, and Calista picked out a turkey sandwich on rye bread. When they finished picking out their food and beverage items and had placed them onto their trays, Dr. Williams paid for both tray contents, and they sat down at a table located in one of the far corners of the cafeteria, safely away from any possible eavesdroppers. They took a few bites before Dr. Williams began to speak.

"So, Calista," he said, "you know that your mother invited me to your Halloween party?"

"Of course!" Calista said. She searched his face. "Why? Are you thinking of declining the invitation?"

"The party's still on?" Dr. Williams asked.

"Of course it is!" said Calista. "What? Do you think that my mother would be the type of person to allow a little murder to mess up her plans?"

"Uh, *three* murders!" said Neville. "And may I remind you that all three of those murders were brutally carried out by some monster who wanted his victims to, before they died, bleed out while suffering excruciating agony at the same time? Calista, this is a dangerous predator who shouldn't be dismissed over a party."

"I know," agreed Calista, "and I appreciate your concern, but those women were only indirectly connected to us because they helped to coordinate the event. The direct connection was their past friendship and social life outside of work. Besides, Mom already hired someone else to plan the party, and there haven't been any more stabbings happening."

"It's only been a few days since the last murder happened," protested Neville. "There could be another murder that will happen tonight, for all we know. Hence, I don't think that the party should go on, but since your mother insists that it is, I am going to show up if only to keep an eye on you."

"Why?" asked Calista.

"For your safety, of course," said Neville.

"What, do you suspect that I'll be the next victim?"

"I did wonder if the three murders were linked to women who were beauties, so yes, I have been worrying about you."

"Aw, that's sweet," said Calista, "but I think that since all three women are the same age, and they all have a past as being emotional Beauties, that it must be someone who had been one of their past victims getting revenge. Although I didn't attend the same elementary schools as they did, I went to the same high school as them. But they were years ahead of me, so we never crossed paths. No, Neville, I think that the motive is personal, and I am not connected in any way to them. I don't even hang out around the nightlife. That's something one would most likely find my brother doing, but I don't think we'll have to worry about him, as far as the idea of males being the target. I really don't think that's the case here."

"One could never practice too much precaution," Dr. Williams warned. "Anyway, since I cannot convince you to persuade your mother in canceling the Halloween party, let's move on to the next subject I wanted to talk to you about." He stopped.

"Yes?"

Dr. Neville Williams cleared his throat. This part of the conversation was definitely more difficult to address.

"I, uh," he began, "I was with Joyce."

"Really?" Calista felt a twinge of jealousy hit her, but soon recovered. She guessed it was because Neville had always seemed to single her out as someone to flirt with, and she had to admit that she felt special over such attention. But the truth was, outside the hospital, Calista didn't know Dr. Williams at all. He could have been married, for all she knew, or had kids. Although he flirted, he never asked her out on a date. Calista figured that his flattering attention had prompted her to develop an illusion, causing her mind to paint a romantic picture of the person Dr. Neville Williams was outside of work. Now, in the few words he had just expressed, she realized that he wasn't that charming doctor who only had eyes for her. *Oh well,* she thought. Her image of him as this dashing, handsome Prince Charming was fun while it lasted. Besides, Calista was beginning to really enjoy her time spent with Fitz, and they seemed to have a lot more in common, which had put her at ease whenever she was around him.

"Yes," answered Neville, sheepishly. "I'm not proud of that fact, but I suppose I could just chalk it up to alcohol mixed with her method of seduction. The problem with Joyce was the fact that she always forgot whom she seduced. And there were a lot of men who fell victim to her charm."

"Why are you telling me this? You should be telling Lieutenant Ram Nandyala or Sergeant Bartholomew Lee. Here"—she reached in the pocket of her nurse's uniform—"I know that I have their cards in here."

Neville reached out and touched her arm to stop her. "It's okay," he said. "I've got their cards, and yes, I did let them know when they questioned me the evening Joyce was brought in. The reason why I'm telling you is because I think of you as more than a fellow employee. I think of you as like a friend."

"I see," said Calista. She took a big bite from her sandwich. It was delicious. The cafeteria at Serowik Hospital was equipped with gourmet chefs who knew how to please every palate that came through there.

"Not only that," continued Neville, "I found out that these women were connected to your family in some sort of manner."

"Where'd you hear that?"

"I think Erin said something to that effect," said Dr. Williams. "The murders have been quite the juicy topic of discussion around here."

Calista took a sip from her drink before asking, "And now that you know a little more of the facts, do you really think that I'm in danger?"

"Like I said before," said Dr. Williams, "one can never practice too much precaution. It's when we let our guards down that we become extremely vulnerable, and bad things are prone to happen." Neville's eyebrows furrowed.

Calista couldn't be certain, but it seemed as if Dr. Williams was keeping something from her, something hidden deep within him, something that might prove to be sinister. She wanted him to tell her, but didn't want to seem impatient, so she said nothing and continued to munch on her sandwich.

"Do the police have any suspects yet?" asked Neville almost too casually.

Calista shrugged, swallowed the contents of her mouth, and said, "I have no idea. They've been around the house a few times, but mentioned nothing about who could have done the murders. I don't even think that they're definite about the motive."

Neville commented, "Mind you, it's definitely anger behind the driving force in these stabbings. The murderer can even be a woman, someone jealous of the three ladies. But what would be the reason behind being so jealous that it would cause one's mind to justify the act of murder?"

"Perhaps the women all slept with some other woman's husband," suggested Calista.

"You know, I hope you don't think that I had a relationship with Joyce nor any of the other women," said Neville.

"But you slept with Joyce," said Calista calmly.

"It was a one-time mistake due to poor judgment and inebriation," admitted Neville.

"Yes, but you did sleep with her all the same," said Calista. "Are you absolutely certain that you didn't have a one-time tryst with Gina or Clara? I mean, you could have been out drinking and had no clue as to who you went to bed with."

Neville stared at Calista. She was hurt, he could tell, but she was inwardly fighting to hide her feelings. Whatever fond feelings he had imagined Calista having toward him before, it was evident to him that this conversation would most certainly squelch that idea.

"No," said Neville, "I'm quite certain that there was nothing between the other two victims and myself."

"Well, that's good for you," said Calista. She stood up abruptly.

"I've got to get going," she said. "I have to get something from my locker before I get back to work." Quickly, Calista picked up her tray and left Dr. Williams alone at the table. He watched her deposit her tray on top of the trash bin and disappear from sight. Was it his imagination, or did she seem disappointed that he admitted to having a fling with the first murder victim?

Chapter 26

The homicide unit of the Temecula Valley Police Department was all abustle with busy officers trying to gather evidence, analyze it, and form various theories that might seem helpful to the investigation. Lieutenant Ram Nandyala and Sergeant Bartholomew Lee hardly slept as they gathered reports from the medical examiner, questioned more witnesses, and looked into the past lives of all three victims including those who came in close contact with those victims. There were some promising leads and some far-fetched, but as far as Ram was concerned, everything needed to be thoroughly examined before any notion of a dismissal.

The two detectives did not often go into Ram's office, but when they did, it was to deposit paperwork and to write out a list of the gathered evidence on the chalkboard. Bartholomew was resting in the leather seat in Ram's office, wishing that the seat were a bed. Ram was getting white powder from the chalk on his right fingers as he wrote on the board.

"From what we had learned so far," said Ram as he wrote key words on the board, "the three women, Joyce Galway, Clara Morton, and Gina Sorenson, were all twenty-five-year-old beautiful women who enjoyed the nightlife, including the company of men, a bit too much. They all knew each other since early childhood, and they were all emotional Bullies, with Joyce as the leader of the group that had caused a lot of damage to many people throughout their years of growing up. Joyce had received a note from a DUB asking her to meet him—or her, for that matter, for it could most definitely be a girl—at the local country western dance club, Scootin' Boots. Joyce must have put the note inside her boot before she went out. As soon as she met up with the mysterious DUB, she was stabbed to death, and no one saw anything definite that points to whom she met. Joyce, still alive and bleeding from her wounds, was taken to the hospital where she died from her injuries. She never had the chance to reveal the name of her attacker."

Ram grabbed a glass of water and sipped it before he continued.

"Our second victim, Clara Morton, was killed at Crystal Chimes. Before she died, she let out an important clue, a girl named Gloria. We figure out that she is this Gloria Wjoinowski, a victim of the Boho Beauties.". Finally, and hopefully with finality, we have our third victim, Gina Sorenson. She was killed in her home. Although she lived alone, she had family whom we notified, and they all said that they have no idea who could have done this to her. We have two very important questions that need to be answered: who and why? Who is the killer, and why were these particular women targeted?"

"I have a question," asked Bartholomew. "Why did the killer wait until the planning of Margaret Serowik's party to begin stabbing these women?"

Ram stopped himself in the middle of writing notes on the board. *Of course,* he said to himself. *That was it!*

Out loud, he exclaimed excitedly, "Bartholomew, you're a genius!"

"I am?" asked Bartholomew, confusion written on his face. "Because of my question, sir?"

"Yes, you see, Bartholomew, you brought us to a very good point. In fact, it's actually a key that opens an important clue." Ram went to his desk, picked up his phone, and dialed.

He repeated Bartholomew's question aloud to himself, "Why *did* the killer wait until the party to begin his killing spree?"

"What's up, sir," said Bartholomew.

"I have to check on a few things first just to confirm," said Ram. "And once we find out for sure, I believe that we'll soon be planning a visit to Margaret Serowik's mansion." His attention returned to the phone.

"Yes, hello?" Ram said. "This is Lieutenant Ram Nandyala. I have a favor to ask you."

Chapter 27

The afternoon marking the anticipated day of Mrs. Margaret Serowik's annual Halloween party had finally arrived. Cars drove through the gates one after another right up to the main driveway where young men, smartly dressed in red jackets and top hats, took over the job of unloading and parking. Two young men took charge of one vehicle at the same time. One young man took the keys to park the vehicle, and the other retrieved the overnight luggage while escorting the guests up to the front entrance. At that point, a man dressed as an old-fashioned English butler greeted them. As soon as the guests identified themselves, the butler instructed the valet personnel on which room to take the guests' personal items.

Every guest was dressed to impress. It seemed that the murder mystery theme inspired many guests to appear in some sort of character from various murder mysteries. So far, the Serowik mansion had welcomed the famous Count Dracula, Frankenstein's monster, and Frankenstein's monster's wife. Richard Serowik was dressed up as Poirot, the famous author Agatha Christie's Belgian detective, equipped with a shiny, perfectly waxed mustache. Margaret was dressed as Jessica Fletcher, the writer/sleuth in the television show, *Murder, She Wrote*. Her hair was curled and coifed above her head, and she wore a conservative flower-print dress along with some sensible black pumps. To make her costume a bit more authentic, she had pinned a vintage typewriter emblem to her dress. Calista was dressed as a sexy Dorothy from *The Wizard of Oz*, and her brother, Connor, looked hilariously accurate in his Columbo costume. Erin Carney, Calista's best friend, and Connor's friend, Jason Thompson, showed up together: Erin as an evil witch, and Jason as the devil. They made quite an adorable pair, Calista thought.

Tables in the front corridor were adorned with various types of delicious appetizers to satisfy anyone's palate. Platters of cheeses, crackers, different creamed dips, pickles, and other relishes made up a small part of the savory spread. To satisfy the sweeter palates, there were platters of cookies, fudge, bite-sized cream-cheese pastries, and tiny cakes, all of which one could handle easily with two fingers. Two bartenders, a man and a woman neatly dressed in crisp white shirts, vests, and ties, stood behind a makeshift bar, and they were busy shoveling ice, mixing, shaking, and pouring to the orders given to them. Calista watched the bartenders fulfill the requests of each guest's choice of spiritual poison and thought to herself, from the way they moved their arms about with such deft skill, that they looked more like carnival jugglers than bartenders.

Hans and Ingaborg were standing together. Ingaborg, tall and erect, held a glass of white wine in her hand and a scowl on her face. She was dressed as the Ice Queen, as she had planned, and her husband looked very handsome and quite muscular dressed as Thor. Hans was holding a tumbler full of amber-colored liquid and was quickly draining its contents. Margaret went to where they were standing and said with her usual sweet welcoming voice, "Ingaborg! And Hans! You both look wonderful! Thank you for coming to my little party. Your floral arrangements give it the perfect accent." She gestured toward the various floral decorations that gave the house a gorgeous pop of color.

Ingaborg's scowl softened a bit from this compliment, but her nose remained positioned high in the air.

"Margaret," she said in a voice that sounded more like a purr, "I simply love your costume as well. Uh, forgive me for asking, but who are you supposed to be?"

"I am the infamous Jessica Fletcher from *Murder She Wrote*," said Margaret with a note of pride in her tone. Then she commented matter-of-factly, "I know that there's nothing really indicative to point to my character since she had so many different outfits in each of her episodes, but I was such a fan of her show as well as the actress, Angela Lansbury, and it seemed perfect to dress as a popular sleuth tonight. I just hope that dressing like her will help me with my detecting skills." She winked at Ingaborg, who gave her a half smile, half wince back.

They chatted for a bit more before Margaret moved on to greet the other guests. Ingaborg, shoulders back, grabbed her husband's arm and led him around the room, making sure that he wouldn't have the chance to wander far from her sight.

Lieutenant Ram Nandyala and Sergeant Bartholomew Lee were one of the first guests to arrive, and they positioned themselves so that they could carefully watch each of the guests as they came into the house and settled themselves socially. Ram was dressed as Sherlock Holmes. Well, he looked more like a Sherlock Holmes who had visited a South American island and had obtained a dark tan. Bartholomew was, of course, Dr. Watson, and looked rather dashing in his brown tweed suit and fake light-brown mustache. Young men and women, whose faces were covered in a white paint to give the appearance of death, were walking around the room, dressed in old-fashioned service uniforms, carrying around silver trays of food and long flutes of champagne for each of the guests to enjoy.

Fitz Palmeri was dressed as James Bond. In order to complete his character, his dark hair was parted on the side and combed in a conservative manner, and he had a 007 pin attached to the lapel of his tuxedo. Calista skipped up to him, looking cute in her Dorothy costume. They hugged. Calista gestured around the room filling up with more guests.

"So what do you think?" she asked.

"It looks amazing," said Fitz. "To say that your mom really goes all out would be a gross understatement!"

After an hour of drinks, small bites, and socializing, everyone had convened in the dining room where they were instructed to find their name tags next to their plates. Underneath some of the name tags lay envelopes, each one addressed to the person's costume character and stamped with red sealing wax. One by one, the guests started to open his or her envelope.

"What are these?" asked Hans as he began opening his envelope addressed to "Thor." He began to read.

"Oh," he said, "it's a little detail about me and about—"

"Shh!" exclaimed Calista while she opened her envelope. "Wait until the murder happens."

As soon as the final guest took his or her seat, the servants had filed into the room with the first course: bowls of soup, split pea, so hot that the steam was visibly rising, delivering an inviting aroma of flavorful warmth and comfort. Baskets of sourdough rolls were served next to small silver saucers of butter. The butter was molded into little skull shapes. The table was set with dark-gray candelabras providing the only type of light, along with the wall sconces set at a very dim setting. A cauldron was placed in the middle of the table containing dry ice. The smoky mist that emanated from the cauldron swirled around the table like an ominous snake looking for something to bite. The mood set at dinner was mysterious. The room looked very haunted. The guests did not say much and silently ate their bread and soup. The second course then came, and servants cleared away the soup bowls making way for other servants to place new platters down in front of each guest. Rosemary-flavored Cornish game hens, covered in a cream-based lemon-and-basil sauce, twice baked potatoes, and roasted carrots were laid before them. The meal was scrumptious, and there was hardly a single plate left unclean. Dessert was simple and refreshing: a single scoop of spumoni was served in a stainless-steel ice cream dish that looked like it had been sitting in a freezer for a while and had accumulated a layer of decorative frost along the exterior of its delicate form.

Everyone sat back in their chairs after they had finished their dessert. Murmurs of absolute praise and congratulations rang out among the guests to their gracious hostess for putting together such a lovely dinner. Margaret stood up, smiled, and absorbed every compliment with gracious ease.

All of a sudden, a crash was heard, then a bone-chilling scream rang out, indicating that it came from somewhere outside the dining room. Every guest ascended from his and her seat, some showing faces of shock and horror, while some looked eager and excited to begin the murder mystery game. The latter also wondered who it was who would be murdered. A maid? One of the guests? Whoever it would be, one thing was certain: the evening's fun had just begun!

The guests all piled out of the dining room, almost tripping over one another toward the terrifying sound they had just heard a few seconds ago. The guests quickly separated themselves into small groups looking all over to where they thought the sound came from, and finally, someone shouted, "Over here!" and everyone responded to the living room. Lying in a twisted heap in front of the large brick fireplace, with her long dark wig draped over her face, a woman dressed to look like Lily Munster from the television comedy show, *The Munsters*, had a large kitchen knife sticking out of her chest and a pool of blood slowly oozing from her pale skin. Shrieks mixed with horror and excitement ejaculated from the guests who were now circling the fake corpse lying before them. Whoever did the makeup work on this woman must have been hired straight out of a Hollywood horror set. Everyone stood stark still, not knowing what to do next.

"Look," someone said. "There's a little piece of paper sticking out of her shoe." Everyone looked to where Cirenio Ulster, dressed as a mummy, was pointing. Partially hidden in the heel of her red platform stilettos was a folded piece of paper. Gingerly, Cirenio picked out the small piece of paper while trying very hard to not step in the pool of fake blood. Unfolding it, he read what was written in a person's handwriting.

"If you value your life, meet me in the living room by the fireplace while dinner is served—M. F. M.," he read aloud.

"What does it mean?" asked Colin O'Darby. He was dressed as Jekyll and Hyde.

"Dinner was served around seven thirty," said Hans, glancing at a tall ornate grandfather clock standing against one of the walls. The clock's shiny brass hands revealed the current time to be eight forty-five. "We were in there for over an hour," he figured, "so she was probably killed somewhere in between those times."

"Well, if she screamed when she was killed, then she was most likely killed just a few minutes ago," said Colin.

Hans slapped the side of his forehead with his right palm and said, "You're right, sorry."

"This can't be the only clue," said Dracula, who was Dr. Neville Williams.

As if on cue, the butler appeared in the doorway of the living room carrying a silver tray with an envelope on it.

"Good evening, ladies and gentlemen," the butler began. "My name is Gerard. Welcome to this year's annual Halloween murder mystery game!" Although his voice escalated into a dramatic volume, his body remained still, making him look the part of absolute sophistication. All the guests watched him as he walked forward and presented the tray with a little bow to a woman playing Ms. Marple.

"My dear Ms. Marple," he said, "will you please do us the honor of reading the next clue?"

"Delighted," giggled the woman. She laid her little bag of knitting—an important accessory of her costume's character—down, took the envelope from the tray, and opened it. She kept the wire-rimmed glasses on her nose as she read,

> In her boudoir you will see
> What this woman used to be
> Was this the reason for the kill?
> Do not waste an act of will.

"I don't think I remember seeing this woman earlier during the party. Where was this woman's room located?" Dr. Williams in his Dracula costume asked.

The butler, who was still lingering nearby, was ready for this question. His face was illuminated by a warm glow coming from the candelabra he gripped in his hand.

"To begin our little murder mystery game, I shall ask those who had received an envelope next to their plates to please return to the dining room and retrieve them. You will need the contents of those envelopes to clear your innocence and to reveal secrets about your fellow suspects."

"Who's our fellow suspects?" asked Neville. The butler ignored this question as everyone grabbed their envelopes and returned to the group.

"This way please, ladies and gentlemen," he said and turned to lead everyone upstairs. Murmurs of excitement came from each of the guests as they followed the butler. When he reached the second floor, the butler continued through the long corridor laden with doors, which led to bedrooms, closets, and bathrooms. The light sconces had been dimmed so low that they gave the hallway a spooky ambience. He stopped in front of one door, opened it, and allowed everyone to gather inside.

Calista wanted to stay as far behind as possible so that she could enjoy the game as more of a spectator than a participant. Since she was the hostess's daughter, she figured that everyone else should be given the better chance to solve the mystery.

The bedroom was designed to look like the boudoir of a female from the 1920s, so to speak. The room was dark except for the soft light emanating from a single lamp on the bedside table. The guests filing into the room caused ominous-looking shadows all over. Rich, deep colors of all different shades appeared throughout the victim's room. The lampshade was the color of crimson fabric and overlapped with black lace. The bed was adorned with a dark-green satin comforter with pillows to match, piled high upon the head. The four-poster bed frame was made of dark mahogany. A vanity of the same dark wood displayed bottles of perfumes, makeup, and gobs of jewelry. Feather boas of many different colors were draped over the mirror above the vanity. The closet, opened so that everyone could see its contents, displayed many different flashy garments and shoes, most likely used for the entertainment of a certain type of paying customer.

"So she was a prostitute?" suggested someone. Everyone agreed that this part was evident.

"The Case of the Murdered Madam of the Night," someone else muttered melodramatically.

"There must be another clue in here," said Connor, cinching up the belt around his tan trench coat. "Everyone, look around for something that'll point to who killed the gothic prostitute."

Everyone was looking furtively for a clue, or at least something that would point to the solution of this game. Christine Ulster, Cirenio's wife, dressed as Cleopatra, looked inside the jewelry box. Nothing was there but a string of costume pearls.

"It kind of looks like she wasn't rich, but she tried to make the room look like she had nice things," said someone.

"Those are my pearls!" exclaimed Erin. Everyone turned to where she was standing. Erin, in her witchy costume, raised her envelope with a green-colored hand.

"It says here that someone stole my pearls, and that they were so valuable that I would kill to get them back!" Her eyes grew wide.

"So you killed her?" asked Colin. His Jekyll and Hyde face looked bummed.

"No, I didn't," Erin said. "But it says that as soon as the pearls are found, I need to clear my innocence by revealing a secret much more relevant to this crime." She paused to look at the text.

"It says that 'Satan seduced her virtue, and when she wanted out, he grew angry and swore revenge.'" Everyone looked toward Jason and his flamboyantly red devil costume.

Jason raised his hands in surrender and grinned. "Hey, wasn't me," he said. "I just seduced her virtue." Some giggled at that remark.

"Can you prove your innocence?" asked Erin. She added a little dramatic emphasis by pointing the end of her broom at him.

Jason looked at the contents of his envelope. "It says that although I wanted to get my revenge, someone else beat me to it. It also says that the victim's lifestyle might help point to the culprit."

The group collectively thought for a few moments. Then a voice called out, "One of the notes said to look at what she used to be. Wait a minute." The voice belonged to Kieran Ryan, dressed as the Wolf Man. He slid his arms underneath the pillows of the bed and searched.

He went on, "Since she was a prostitute and the bed is where she entertained, then who she was and what she did for a living would mostly be done in her bed, right?" He stopped moving his arms and extracted from underneath one of the pillows another piece of folded paper. Everyone gathered as close to him as possible as he read,

> Consider the method used upon me
> Keep your mind as sharp as can be
> Do not stray from the pointed goal
> The answer will soon be easy to behold.

"What do you think that means?" asked someone.

"It has to be the kitchen, came a reply. It was Christine Ulster.

"Since the method used to kill her was a pointy knife," she reasoned, "and we have to keep our minds 'as sharp as can be,' it's got to be the knife, and that most likely came from the kitchen."

Everyone, satisfied with this suggestion, piled back through the corridor, down the stairs, and made their way to the kitchen. The kitchen was a replicated version of every chef's dream. It was large and spacious. The whole place was neatly organized and clean. The counters were made of navy-blue granite, and on top of them lay every modern gadget and cooking tool needed to produce any type of creative concoction. Copper pots and pans with wooden handles hung in order of size on a pot rack attached to the ceiling above the island. Both the freezer and the pantry were walk-ins, stocked high with food and various kinds of necessary ingredients to feed an army of people.

It didn't take long for everyone to spot the missing knife from the wooden knife block. Obviously, the missing knife would end up being the murder weapon. Poking out from the slot where the knife should have been was a third folded piece of paper. This time, a man dressed as a mime picked the piece of paper out and unfolded it. His eyes glanced over the words before he handed the paper to Hans's character, Thor. Hans read the words out loud,

> Congratulations.
> You've arrived where the killer stole the deadly tool.
> A clue for you to manage
> Find out which among you is the guilty fool.
> Good luck with your challenge!

Everyone was silent, and they all seemed to think at once as to what to do, but were unsure as to whether or not they should voice it. Jason, in his devil's costume, said, "Well? Where do we go from here?"

"We could go back to the body to see if there's something we missed," suggested Colin in his Jekyll and Hyde costume.

They went to the area in the living room where they left the body of the so-called dead woman. The "corpse" was still lying in the same place. As they stared both at her body and around the room, some noted that the "dead" woman was getting a bit uncomfortable as she let out an occasional twitch, probably from a muscle spasm.

"Let's look at the angle of the knife," said Ingaborg, pointing a long slim finger at the weapon sticking out of the prostitute's chest. "The knife is positioned on the left side of her chest, pointing at a downward forty-five-degree angle, suggesting that the killer was taller than the woman and that the killer held the knife gripped in his right fist." She positioned her own hand with her fingers pointing down and her thumb pointed towards the ceiling to show an example of how the killer could have held the knife.

"So if she was standing when she was stabbed, the culprit is most likely someone taller than our dead girl," said Connor. He stuck his hands in the pockets of his trench coat. "It could be a man or a woman, I suppose. I mean, look at the dead lady. She's pretty petite from what I can see, and most of the women here are taller than her. For example, look at Ice Queen here." He placed his hand on Ingaborg's shoulder to indicate how tall she was.

"What are you?" he asked, "Five foot eleven? Six feet?"

Ingaborg shrugged his hand off her shoulder, and her icy glare made him put up his hands in defense. "Hey," he said, "you're the one who proved that the stabbing had to be done by a tall person."

"So why pick on me," retorted Ingaborg. "There are plenty of other tall people here who could have killed her."

"Yeah, but none of them here can match your absolutely charming personality," whispered Erin to Calista. Though she spoke under her breath, Erin could feel Ingaborg's steel eyes on her.

"Besides, I can prove my innocence," Ingaborg screeched. She waved her long thin arm as she shook her envelope in Connor's Columbo-like face. Connor blinked and instinctively shooed her hand away.

Ingaborg read, "It says here that I hated the victim because she stole the only man I've ever loved: Count Dracula! But I didn't kill her. My father can attest to that." She looked at the text before her and continued. "It says here that my father and mother are Frankenstein's Monster and Frankenstein's Monster's Wife."

"It's true," both Frankenstein's Monster and his wife said in unison. Frankenstein's Monster's Wife continued, "We were all in the backyard roasting marshmallows around a fire pit."

"The three of you?" asked Fitz.

"The three of us," answered Monster's Wife.

"There's tea set for two here," said Christine Ulster. She moved gracefully in her Cleopatra's costume to a small coffee table in the room. A complete tea tray was displayed with two cups. The contents of one of the cups was halfway drunk and the print of a deep shade of red lipstick left by someone's mouth showed along the rim. The other cup was still filled to the rim, indicating that its contents had not been touched.

"So someone, this mysterious M. F. M., sent her a note to meet him, or her, here in the living room," said Jason. "That person had tea prepared for them both. The killer probably wanted to simply talk to her in a civilized manner." He gestured with his red pitchfork back toward the "body" and continued.

"But something happened," he figured. "Heated words were said, and the killer decided to kill the woman!"

"The problem with that theory," said the mummified Cirenio, "is that, if the killer prepared the tea to talk in a civil manner and was expecting the conversation to be just that, perfectly civilized, he wouldn't have been prepared with a knife."

Jason said, "Okay, so the killer did expect to end her life, but why bring tea if murder was the ultimate end?"

Erin Carney, in her witch's costume, spoke up, "Smoke screen? Maybe he wanted to get her off her guard—although I should use the pronoun *she*. The tea gives a feminine touch to the murder. She was probably suspicious at first, but when she saw that the killer only wanted to have a cup of tea with her and talk, well then, that would have soothed matters. What we could do is go back to her room and get a deeper look at who she was, who she dealt with, who gained by her death, and stuff like that."

"I guess so," agreed Cirenio. "There doesn't seem to be anything else down here. We can always return if we can't find anything up there."

"Why don't we split up in three groups and look here, up in her room, and the kitchen?" The voice came from the mime, and everyone threw him an astonished look. "Oh please," he said, folding his arms. "There's a murder that just happened. That'll scare the silent out of anybody." That brought a chuckle among the guests.

Dr. Williams said, "I'll go upstairs to the kitchen. Who's with me?"

"I'll go," said Connor, Jason, and Erin at the same time. They all looked at one another and giggled.

"We'll go too," said Cirenio, putting an arm, completely wrapped in yellowish-white bandages, around his Egyptian queen. Christine nodded.

Fitz said, "I'll take the kitchen. Who wants to come along there?"

"Me," said Calista eagerly. She skipped over to Fitz's side, and they grinned at each other. Neither of them saw the pained look of dejection written on Neville Williams's face.

Colin and Kieran agreed to go too. So did the mime and Ms. Marple.

Frankenstein, his wife, and Hans and Ingaborg said that they would remain in the living room with the "body" and look further for something that might be a clue.

It was decided among the guests that they would reconvene in the dining room in half an hour to share notes.

The bedroom was still the same, and Calista wondered how on earth they would find something relevant to the game. She decided that being more of a spectator would not help much since she had no idea of how the murderous game was planned out before the party. Her mother really did keep it hushed. Where were Mother and Father, she thought. For that matter, where were the lieutenant and the sergeant? They seemed to just disappear, probably during the commotion of hearing the scream and finding the body. Calista wondered if they all collaborated together to create this evening's murder. It was, in fact, a crude reenactment of the recent murders of the three beautiful women. Was the lieutenant trying to use tonight's game to help him figure out the killer of his real-life mystery? *That would seem quite humorous,* she thought with amusement. But then again, she also realized, Lieutenant Ram Nandyala was a bit unconventional, a man who marched to the beat of his own tune, and that tune had a certain organized precision to it. *That particular fact is most likely the secret to his success,* she told herself. Calista knelt down and looked under the bed, since everyone else in her group had picked out the most obvious items to look through. Fitz had the side table. He opened the drawer and looked inside. Nothing was in there. Kieran and Colin went through the closet, studying different garments and shoes, looking for anything out of the ordinary. So far, nothing seemed amiss. The mime opened and looked through the vanity. He opened the various glass bottles on the table and smelled the contents to see if there might be some suspicious odor in them. He made a circle with his thumb and first finger and ran the feather boas one by one through the circle.

Calista couldn't find anything important underneath the bed, so she got up and looked around the room. Behind her was a dresser with five drawers. She called Fitz over, who helped her look through the contents of each drawer. The top drawer was full of scarves and gloves. The second drawer was full of different kinds of underwear: silky panty hose, laced panties and bras, and a black corset. The tags on the lingerie read "Fifi's," which was a high-end lingerie shop that sold only the best sexy underwear. Tucked in the back corner of the underwear drawer was a pile of envelopes, neatly stacked and wrapped in a single red ribbon. Calista gave out an excited squeal, which brought everyone else to see what she found. Calista held up her discovery and went over to the bed so that everyone could inspect it.

When she untied the ribbon, she handed an envelope to each person in the group to read. All of the envelopes had the name *Evelyn* written on them in different styles of handwritings. She opened her envelope and began to read out loud.

"Dear Evelyn," Calista read. "Last night was wonderful. Your blood was sweet and delicious. Can't wait for next time. Love, Dracula."

Fitz read the contents of the envelope in his hand. "My darling Evelyn, when shall I see you again? I long for the way you feel when you pet me. Kisses, Wolfman."

Colin giggled a little before he read the letter in his envelope. "'Dearest Evelyn, selling a body as beautiful as yours is a crime. Leave your life of ill repute and marry me. I'll take care of you. Love always, Poirot.' Oh, this is hilarious!" He bellowed with laughter.

"Ha ha!" exclaimed Connor. "My dad's Poirot, and I don't think that my mom's character, Jessica Fletcher, will be pleased to know that he's been carrying on with a prostitute." Calista smiled at this.

They opened the rest of the envelopes and read the remaining letters. They were all the same, indicating that Evelyn had had rendezvous with each of the male guests at the party.

"How did they know what we were going to be?" asked the mime, who was also named as one of Evelyn's occasional companions.

"They probably prepared the notes while we were at dinner so as to implicate all male guests as suspects," said Colin.

"But the killer could have been a woman as well," said Connor. "The killer does know who he or she is, right? I mean, one of the guests here has to act like he or she is a detective figuring this game out and at the same time knows that it's him or her who is the chosen killer of the game, right? It's not like I'm the killer and I've got to figure out from the clues that I am the culprit? It would seem more probable that I would be informed before the party, then I'd have to act like I have no clue until the end."

"I believe so," said Calista. "But Mom didn't go over the rules with me, so I'm not sure. We'll just have to look at all the clues in order to sum up who the real murderer is, but also keep in mind that the clues could point to ourselves."

They agreed to this and looked at the face of a small antique clock located on the side table, next to the lamp. The time indicated that a half hour had gone by, so they walked down to the dining room, and each took a seat. The rest of the party soon filed in and did the same. All guests looked at each other wondering who should start first. Finally, Dr. Williams spoke up, "My group and I have just finished scouring the kitchen, and we have found something that seems like an interesting clue." He produced a note written with large letters that had been cut out of magazines and pasted onto the paper that read, "You'll never get away with telling her our secret!" It was unsigned.

"Where did you find that?" asked Ms. Marple.

"Inside the broom closet," answered Neville.

Calista then produced the evidence from her group. After she passed around each of the letters, the guests were even more excited. They had some of the pieces and had to figure out where they fit in the puzzling game. Now they were getting closer to solving the mystery.

Finally, all attention was focused on the group that stayed in the living room: Ms. Marple, Frankenstein's Monster, Frankenstein's Monster's Wife, Hans as Thor, and Ingaborg as the Ice Queen produced their clue. It was also a piece of paper, rolled up with a poem written on it. Rolled in the paper, also, was a black rose. Ingaborg in her sparkling costume read the poem to everyone present.

> The clues are there, but can you tell
> What the motive is as well?
> Is it revenge? Is it rage?
> A split-second notion or planned for an age?
> You might be worried how complicated this looks
> When, really, it's as simple as a fairy-tale book.

"Fairy tale," repeated Jason. His devilish face frowned in concentration, making his countenance look menacing.

"And it's simple, not complicated," said Cirenio. "But it doesn't seem simple to me. I'm confused."

"Why don't we just go around the room and ask each other if we are the killer?" suggested the Mime.

"Really? That would be cheating," retorted Erin, her green face scowling at the mime. "Besides, what fun would it be for us if we don't take the time to figure it out? The clues are here, and we just have to put our heads together and review each item to solve the mystery."

Jason said, "We should also keep in mind that it could be the least likely person. The killer is usually the least likely person to commit murder in most mystery novels."

"Me too," said Calista. She rested her chin in the cups of her hands and closed her eyes. Suddenly, her eyes widened.

"Wait! I've got it!" she called out triumphantly. Everyone paused and waited for her to continue.

"Well, I'm not certain who the culprit is yet, but I do have an idea. Listen, it started with a scream, a murder, and a list of clues to get everyone's emotions up and scattered in all different directions. We're all trying to figure out this game while being distracted by all the excitement of the evening. It's like we're all just waiting to be spoon-fed the next clue and the next until the conclusion is revealed to us without any of us figuring it out for ourselves. But the truth is, it's not going to be revealed by someone. We have to figure out the killer's identity ourselves."

Calista left the dining room momentarily and returned with a notebook. "Okay," she said, "let's all take a deep breath and go over each clue thoroughly. Number one, the killer's initials are M. F. M. Number two, the killer is taller than our victim, after looking at the angle of the knife driven in the woman's body. Number three, the killer prepared tea before killing the victim. Number four, the victim was a prostitute. Number five, there are love notes from every male character at the party. Number six, there's a clue in the broom closet saying that the victim won't get away with telling a 'her' a secret. The note in the pantry made it seem like someone was enacting revenge upon the prostitute for telling 'her,' but who is this woman referred to as 'her'? She didn't think that there was going to be any danger meeting up with M. F. M., and she still didn't seem to think that there was any danger as she sipped her tea, so the heated confrontation must have happened well into the meeting."

The mime said, "So the prostitute, Evelyn, said something to another woman, and that something had caused hurt upon the other woman, something that the killer did not want known, and so Evelyn ended up paying the ultimate price for opening her big mouth."

Erin asked, "So what kind of secret would qualify a death sentence to the person who revealed it? She was a prostitute, so it probably had to do with sex. She might have told the wife of one of her lovers, which would hurt the wife a lot, and cause a lot of harm to the marriage. That's certainly a motive."

Kieran said, "Well, if the wife already knows about Evelyn's involvement with her husband, then why kill her?"

"Maybe that wasn't the initial intention," said Colin, his face half painted as a grotesque monster while the other half was left alone to show the mild-mannered Dr. Jekyll part of his character. "Maybe he tried to reason with her, to get her to tell the wife that she was lying about the husband's involvement with her, and Evelyn refused to do so. The conversation got heated, she said something that angered him, and he just stabbed her."

Christine asked, "How did he get the knife in the first place? Did he bring it with the tea things and hide it from view just in case he might need it?"

"Could be," said Cirenio. "The subject of the meeting was a delicate one. We're talking about infidelity and the potential breakup of a marriage. She could make things much worse for the husband's relationship with his wife. Maybe she fell in love with M. F. M. and pestered him to leave his wife for her. Therefore, M. F. M. figured that the only way to get her off his back was to kill her."

"I've got it!" shouted Fitz. His arms shot up like a runner passing through the ribbon at the finish line, and his appearance looked very authoritative in his James Bond costume. He practically jumped from his chair out of excitement. "M. F. M. is obviously the abbreviation of the name of the killer, and since we're dealing with character's names from our Halloween costumes instead of our real names, then it's simple to decipher that the killer is none other than Mister Frankenstein's Monster, and the 'her' referred to in the letter found in the kitchen is Frankenstein's Monster's Bride!" Everyone held his or her breath. The room was absolutely silent.

All of sudden, the tall green figure of Frankenstein's Monster shot up from where he sat. His eyes were wild with rage, and after reaching into the tattered jacket, which was part of his costume, he pulled out a gun and pointed it toward the shocked guests. Frankenstein's Bride screamed and tried to reach for her husband. Frankenstein's Monster used his free arm to stop her and returned his attention to the rest of the room's occupants.

Frankenstein's Monster glared at Fitz with a menacing look.

"How did you figure me out?" he asked Fitz.

Fitz swallowed and cleared his throat. "Well, I figured that your initials had to be something a little more complicated, and adding the title of Miss or Mister would have to be the answer. Then your alibi didn't seem to add up. When you said that you were out with your wife around the fire, I knew that couldn't be the truth. You see, Frankenstein's Monster could not go near fire since that was the only weapon that could possibly kill him."

"Bravo!" cheered Connor. He directed a short applause at Fitz.

With a snarl in his tone, Frankenstein's Monster said, "So you have figured out the identity of Evelyn's real killer. I was afraid that one of you would figure it out. How unfortunate it was that I missed the various clues that were scattered around the house, but now that I have all of the evidence here in one place,"—he gestured toward the contents brought in by guests—"I'll simply confiscate all of which could point to me as the culprit." Then he shouted "Don't move!" at the guests, who all sat stark still around the table, watching Frankenstein's Monster with wide eyes and open mouths. Thoughts passed through the minds of the guests. Each of them wondered if the performance before them was real or just a very good example of theatrical genius.

After Frankenstein's Monster gathered up the items that were considered evidence and placed them in the pockets of his jacket, the big green figure of the monster slowly and methodically retreated from the room, his gun still pointed toward the guests, daring them to move a muscle. Not one person moved a muscle. They all glanced at one another with looks of fright written on their faces. Frankenstein's wife called out to her husband.

"Please, my love," she cried, pleading with him, "take me with you!" The other guests looked at her with wide-eyed astonishment. Was she really begging to accompany the killer? Never mind the fact that he was her husband. The monster was a killer!

Frankenstein's Monster looked as if he was going to tell her no, but instead, he said, still in his monster-like voice, "Oh, very well! Come, my wife."

She leapt from her chair and stood next to his side. Her movement had caused the massive curly bouffant atop her head to bounce unsteadily. Her husband told her to go through the dining room door and ordered her to get their car ready at the front door so that they could make their getaway. Frankenstein's Monster's Bride retreated. Frankenstein's Monster walked stealthily backward toward the same door that his wife went through, and keeping his gun pointed towards the group of seated guests, he said, "If any of you dares to follow me, I am prepared to shoot!" Then quick as a flash, Frankenstein's Monster had disappeared through the door.

The remaining occupants were still seated, clearly unknowing what to do at that moment. They shared frightened stares with each other, but no one spoke a word, since there didn't seem to be anything to say.

Suddenly, as if on cue, the sound of a single person clapping could be heard, breaking the silence of the current atmosphere. Stunned, the guests turned to see Lieutenant Ram Nandyala in his Sherlock Holmes costume standing now in the doorway, applauding with enthusiasm. Behind him stood Sergeant Bartholomew Lee, and the two detectives proceeded toward the sitting guests. They stood at the head of the dining room table and took in the astonishing expressions looking back at them. A moment went by, and Richard and Margaret Serowik walked in, arm in arm. They chose two empty seats next to each other and sat down. Margaret's face was beaming. It was clear that the woman was proud of the outcome produced so far at her party.

"First," Ram began, addressing the group of people seated, "let me congratulate Mr. James Bond, the winner of our murder mystery, for using his efficient skills of detection to solve the heinous crime committed tonight. I can assure you that the death of our dear Lady of the Night will not have been in vain and that justice will prevail. Ladies and gentlemen, our murder victim, Evelyn!"

The actress who played Evelyn walked in, still showing her pasty white skin, most likely body makeup, and a little of the blood still lingering on her chest. She had removed the knife before she entered the dining room. Everyone clapped as Evelyn gave a little curtsy.

"And a big thank you to our murderer!" Ram lifted his arm toward the door to greet the big green monster that looked positively different from the character that, just a few moments ago, had pointed a threatening weapon at them. Frankenstein's Monster and his wife marched back into the room with such a theatrical entrance. As rehearsed, the two actors bowed with such a dramatic flair that thoroughly impressed their audience. Laughs and hoots roared from the guests as the two divas took their bow. Everyone seemed to thoroughly enjoy the game as well as the delivery of entertainment. Despite the setback of three real-life murders that were previously connected to it, this party was a true success, Margaret could see, and she was beaming deeply with pride.

The servants who had disappeared during the game were now reappearing one by one through the swinging door that separated the dining room from the kitchen. Looking like marching penguins, they filed in and stood shoulder to shoulder along the walls behind the seated guests. As they filed in, they also joined in the applause. It was truly a joyous scene.

When the cheery noise had died down, Lieutenant Ram Nandyala held up his hand and announced, "And now, ladies and gentlemen, the evening's not yet finished. In fact, it has only begun, for we still have another mystery to solve this evening."

The guests exchanged nervous glances among themselves. Something in the lieutenant's tone didn't seem like it was part of the act. The look in his eyes was strictly serious.

Ram continued, "I must confess that I am the amateur mastermind behind this party's little puzzle. I say amateur generously because I have never organized a fake murder mystery before in my life. I am, however, an expert when it comes to real murder, and so

I applied those skills to this little act for the evening. I must admit that even an expert professional such as myself can become stumped, no matter how much practice he or she has experienced in his or her lifetime. Sometimes it is difficult to overcome that obstacle-riddled stump no matter how many resources one has. Tonight's puzzling fun includes some of the minute complications that I have been facing recently while trying to solve the murders of our three local women who originally were supposed to be involved with tonight's entertainment. At first, I was so caught up in the various developments that arose in this case taking me toward different theoretical paths that I failed to see the simplicity of it. In order to make the case less complicated for my esteemed colleague, Sergeant Lee, and myself, the motive had to be clear. And through much research and going over all the notes located in the case file, I was, at last, able to pinpoint the motive. You see, it was all about the motive, or the underlining reason for these murders that held the key to solving them. The motive is such a powerful key to obtain since it cuts out all the unnecessary fat and reveals the bare bones of the murder.

"I must admit that some of you here tonight took turns being number one on my suspect list while some of you did not fall far behind. I thought at first that Hans Krause could have committed Joyce's murder since he was having an affair with her. Since I am speaking with absolute frankness in front of all of you tonight, Hans had many different affairs with many different women. Joyce was simply one of many, I knew. But then I came across a very important piece of evidence that forced me to realize that Joyce was someone very different for Hans. Hans, being a good-looking man with a good physique and sexual appeal, has no problem picking up women and, once conquering them, gets tired easily of their attention. However, Joyce was a unique person altogether. In her, Hans had met his ultimate match.

"Despite the fact that she was small, Joyce has had this strong innate ability to dominate men and bring them to their knees for her. Someone joked to me once saying that Joyce had never known what it was like to open a single door for herself. In a sense that was true. She exhumed a certain type of feminine magic that men found too strong to resist. Men tripped over their own shoes to do even the smallest favors for her, such as opening a door for her. It is this type of magic that very few women possess, and when men do come across this particular type of woman, it is difficult to hold on to one's own sexual control. This is what happened to Hans. He saw a beautiful woman, put the moves on her, as he did with most women he encountered, and had her. But to his surprise, the outcome hit him with complete surprise. Instead of him having her, it was she who had him, and Hans could not help himself but fall in love, true love, and to his ultimate dismay, it was a feeling that was not reciprocated by Joyce. To me, this type of love, so strong, so inflamed, could also be turned into sparks of hatred, so inflamed that the only relief to his problem would be to kill the one person who had him 'by the balls,' so to speak. But if Joyce was the only death, I would have looked even closer at Hans. However, she was just the first of three, and I found that the other two victims, although beautiful in their own right, did not hold the same influence over men. Clara and Gina had that outside appeal that intrigued men at first glance, but they did not have that inward ability of influence like Joyce Galway did.

"For the same reasons that I suspected Hans Krause, I also thought that Ingaborg Krause could have killed Joyce. It would make sense if one looked at the situation from the angle that a jealous wife acted upon revenge against the woman who was able to steal, not only her husband's body, but his heart and soul as well. However plausible this theory is, she wouldn't have had a motive for killing Clara nor Gina, since Hans couldn't even remember if he had been with either of the two latter women, so as I did with her husband, I crossed Ingaborg off of my list of suspects." Ram ignored the frigid blue darts ejecting from the Ice Queen's eyes. Obviously, she did not enjoy this raw revelation of herself as being seriously suspected.

"I also had to look at the two friends, Colin O'Darby and Kieran Ryan, who had, ahem, a most intimately wild time with both Joyce and Clara. However, I soon had to eliminate them since they didn't seem to feel something deeper than acquaintance with the first two victims. Plus, they both had alibis, and their only major crime was the breaking of many girls' hearts." Colin and Kieran shared a glance between themselves; they grinned and gave each other a quick fist bump.

"I also thought that maybe Connor Serowik could have been the killer, since all three victims were involved with his mother's party. He had access to all women involved, he was guilty of being a chronic partyer, so he must have come across each of them at some point. But just like Colin and Kieran, his only crime is being a playboy, and he also has an alibi during the murders."

Connor raised both his arms, palms up, and sang, "Thank the good Lord, Jesus!"

"Amen," added Calista. "I'm not too keen on the idea of visiting you in prison." Connor smiled and stuck his tongue out at his sister.

Ram continued, "I also thought that Dr. Neville Williams could have possibly been a suspect. As far as Joyce was concerned, Dr. Williams had been bitten by her charming disposition, and it stung when he realized that he was just a simple notch in her belt. But that theory was soon eliminated since he was at the hospital while Joyce and the other two victims were wheeled in, and after I looked into it, there was no way he could have left the hospital before then to meet up with and stab the victims."

"Very gracious of you," said Dr. Williams with a tone of cynicism in his voice. Ram ignored his sarcasm.

"Of course," said Ram, smiling down at Calista, "Calista Serowik did not seem to have any connection to the murders and was also at the hospital working while Joyce and Clara were murdered. Plus, she had no idea who the victims were before her mother hired Joyce as the event coordinator."

"Then there's Christine Ulster, who knew all three victims. She was once one of the infamous Boho Beauties that terrorized those around them during their childhood. But what would the motive be for Christine wanting them dead? She had her own life, a husband, and she says that she didn't know Joyce was still around until she saw her at the Serowik's house. As soon as she did see Joyce, she practiced caution around the woman and was nervous about her husband working around them, knowing Joyce's unrelenting powers of seduction, but other than that, there is no real reason to want Joyce or the other women dead."

"Then there is Fitz Palmeri, who tended to the victims after they were stabbed. But looking into his background, I found no personal connection with any of the three women. Besides, Fitz was younger than the women murdered, and he grew up in a different town, so it was easy to eliminate him."

Ram paused and closed his eyes for a moment before he continued, "I must admit that the motive had me absolutely baffled. I didn't know whether to think the killer was a disgruntled lover, a jealous woman, a crazed serial killer, or someone who fell victim to her youthful bullying. There were so many different tangents to lead me in various directions, and the more I searched, the more the case became a twisted labyrinth for me. There was one idea about this case that I could be sure about, and that was that the killer knew each one of the victims. How well or how little would have to be determined, but the killer knew them. That was for certain.

"Then I came up with the idea that this case, although seemingly complex, could actually be the opposite. So I mentally stepped outside of myself wrapped up in the complexities of the case and decided to look at the situation with a new manner of thinking. Out of the three victims, the one who stood out the best was Joyce Galway. Joyce was selfish and egotistical, but she was most importantly a leader to the group of girls that she associated herself with. She was more than a leader though. In the same sense that she possessed this innate ability to influence men, she could do the same with women. She was a controller. And that is a very powerful force that one person can possess. How that person uses that power can dictate the outcome of that person's fate. Although Clara Morton and Gina Sorenson were part of the Boho Beauties, they did not have the same kind of disposition that Joyce Galway had. They were instead followers, and although they were just as guilty as Joyce was, when it came to bullying, they were only two of the tools that she used to carry out her orders. I do believe that they did have a mean streak, and that is what attracted them to follow under Joyce, but I also believe that if they didn't have Joyce as their mastermind, Clara and Gina would not have done all of those horrible deeds. It was meeting Joyce and following her instruction that started a series of cruel deeds. Therefore, years later, because of their association with Joyce as their ringleader, the girls ended up murdered as well.

"When I looked at the fact that the stabbings had everything to do with the past instead of now, things started to fall into place for Sergeant Lee and me. Maybe one of the victims still held a grudge all these years. From that idea, a good question came up that was presented to me: 'Why begin to kill these women now?' and that got me to think even more outside that box. Why *now?* That seemed to be very important. It's been eight years since Joyce, Clara, and Gina graduated from high school, and even more years since they started their acts of bullying. Did the killer decide to take advantage of a Halloween party in order to add to the sinister ambience of the holiday? Why choose this year instead of the years past? Perhaps the killer didn't know where the Boho Beauties had gone after high school. After all, Joyce herself was in Los Angeles for years before she came back home to start her own business and recruit some of her old school buddies as employees.

"Once she came back, she had been working in Temecula for a little over a year before getting the Serowik Halloween party venue. It wasn't until then that she was stabbed, and a note pointing toward the killer's signature as DUB was found in the heel of her boot. The note alone indicates that the murder was personal, and the multiple stab wounds inflicted only confirmed that theory. I was then brought to question the killer. What if the killer's motive wasn't directly related to the murder victims, but instead indirectly related? I've already established that the killer knew each of the victims, but what if the killer was only related to the people whom the Boho Beauties hurt? The only problem is that we don't know who DUB is. Then Clara is murdered in the same manner at Crystal Chimes, a popular night-club, but no note was found on her. Her death could have been a random killing except for the fact that she knew Joyce, worked with Joyce, and had a past with Joyce. The same goes for Gina. She was not killed in a local nightclub or bar, but she died in the same manner as Clara and Joyce, stabbed over and over again, which pointed to emotional rage coursing through the killer's veins. Therefore, we have three murders, all connected, and all supposedly committed by DUB. Still, the question remains, who is DUB?

"At first, I thought the signature was either a code or a set of initials that were those of a person's first and last name, and it was driving me crazy having to eliminate all of these possible suspects whose initials were DUB. That task in itself was tiring, but thankfully, I have a highly trained staff that is prepared for extensive and efficient research.

"After a while, my team came up with nothing promising, which prompted me to return to my office and once again think outside the box. What if DUB stood for something more than just initials? DUB could be short for someone's name, like Dudley or Dublin. But even that didn't seem to fit. It did, however, offer me ideas to work on. Ultimately, that drove me to wonder about the relationship between Joyce and her killer as being the same as by a student and her teacher, so I decided to take a trip down to the Everest High School for a chat with the principal, who then directed me to the office staff. A very nice lady named Mrs. Snyder had been working as an office clerk for the past fifteen years. She knew all of the staff members at Everest High and was very helpful with the information that I sought.

"It seems that there was a certain librarian, well-known among the students, who was well liked because she was so nice to everyone. She was known as an understanding woman because she allowed a lot of students to return their overdue books without owing any fees. She was also one of the first to volunteer big contributions to bake sales. She would make tons of baked goods and even give some away to students, especially the popular ones. Joyce was an often recipient of her baked goods.

"The librarian had an unusual last name, *Wjoinoski*, pronounced Hoy-now-skee, and it was a bit difficult for some to remember the spelling. Teenagers are known to, at times, come up with their own little unique ways to address their elders. For those adults they don't like, they come up with names of a negative nature like Ms. Piggy Face or Mr. Banana Pants when they refer to that adult during conversations. For those adults whom they really like, they don't have a pet name to replace the conventional ways to address a Mr. Smith or Mrs. Walker. That would seem childish to an adolescent who is determined to look cool in any given situation. It seems to be the fashion today for teens to use words or names that they find favor in with a shorter, more simplified way of saying that word or name. For example, nowadays, teenagers who want to express the phrase 'totally fabulous' would simply say 'totes fab.' It's like when kids thought something was really great or fantastic, they would simply say 'cool' to voice their compliments. In this particular case with the librarian, the students started to call her by a more simplified name: Mrs. W. After some time, the name Ms. W. just stuck. Then the initial 'double-you' was too long to pronounce, so the kids shortened the letter's sound to 'dub,' making the librarian's new name sound like Ms. Dub. This not only stuck, it was quite popular, and everyone, including other staff members, began calling her that. Her original nameplate that sat on her desk in the library was replaced one year with one that read 'Ms. Dub.' Over time, some even forgot Ms. Dub's real last name since she was only known by the student-christened term.

"I thought that the initials on the note, Ms. DUB, was a bit far-fetched to think that it stood for Mrs. W., but I was informed by those who were at Everest High School during the years that she was working there, that this short nickname for the librarian was so popular that the librarian eventually signed all of her notes with a Ms. DUB or just simply DUB, and not Mrs. Wjoinowski. It was very important that the initials Ms. DUB were a common occurrence for her to use, and it was important for me to see exactly how often she signed Ms. DUB and, most importantly, if seeing Ms. DUB, Joyce would know exactly whom it was that sent the note. This was quite an exciting breakthrough for me in this case since it seemed to lead me to the next step. I had to find out who this Ms. DUB was and how she became Joyce Galway's, Clara Morton's, and Gina Sorensen's killer.

"From more extensive research into her personal life, I found that this particular librarian also had a daughter who went to high school at the same time that Joyce, Clara, and Gina attended Everest High. The daughter's name was Gloria Wjoinowski, and the bullying that she endured was so extreme it eventually caused her to land into a rehab center in the unhealthiest state of being. Gloria didn't graduate from high school, and her condition was devastating for both her and her mother. Gloria's mother had to pick up another job of cleaning houses just to help pay for her daughter's rehab, and soon she had to quit her library job in order pick up more cleaning jobs, some that required her to work at odd hours of the morning and evening. Gloria's mother did everything she could to help her daughter, but then Gloria disappeared out of the blue, and her mother never heard from her again. Gloria's mother couldn't return to her library job at the school and had to continue working in domestic service. Isn't that correct, Mrs. Connie Wjoinowski? Or should I say, Ms. DUB?"

Everyone's eyes shifted automatically toward where Ram had directed his inquiry: the Serowik's cook, Connie. The woman was alone, standing in her little corner of the wall. Her eyes met with Ram's, and the message that those eyes were saying could not be interpreted by any onlooker, and yet one could definitely tell that there was no hostility written on her face after being called out on the carpet, so to speak. On the contrary, there seemed to be this shade of relief that instantly washed over her whole body. Her shoulders slackened a bit, but her head remained high as if to show that she still held the pride and dignity of whom she was and what she'd done.

Connie said, her voice escalating and strong, "Gloria was my daughter. She was my baby girl, and those sick fiends ruined her life! They were more than fiends. Those Beauties were absolute monsters. They destroyed my girl's dreams, her desires, her future, her entire soul, and all because it felt good to them to break other people."

"Oh, Connie," whispered Margaret sympathetically. She tried to get up from her chair, but her husband placed a firm hand on her arm to stop her. Margaret looked at her husband's understanding but firm expression and decided that he was right to keep her seated.

Connie said, "My daughter was such a lovely, happy child. She was also shy and quiet and loved to read. She used to tell me that reading books allowed her to pretend that she was a part of the stories and that the characters in the books were her friends. She was comfortable with that kind of social life because she said that imag-

179

inative friends never laugh at you nor do they criticize any awkward behavior that you may display. And my dear Gloria did have her little awkward quirks, which made her even more lovable."

Ram nodded his head in understanding. She sensed this, and her voice grew louder with confidence as she continued.

"She was genuine, truthful, and sweet. And then she entered into high school. I didn't think to take much mind to the usual changes of puberty. We all had to go through that uncomfortable stage in our lives, so I expected the natural changes to occur in Gloria as well. It never occurred to me that Gloria was enduring bullying on top of the normal awkwardness of being a teenager. That is, it never occurred to me until it was too late, and she was so far gone. Gloria never uttered a word of what was going on at school. She stopped eating and lost a tremendous amount of weight. When I tried to get her to eat, she would pretend to comply, but as soon as my back was turned, she'd discard the food in any way she could. If she had already eaten a few bites, she'd use the toilet to get rid of the contents. She started using drugs in order to dull the pain she was enduring from those wicked girls. Then she began to mix alcohol with those drugs to bring on the dull euphoria at a quicker pace. To me, it seemed like it all happened overnight. One day, she was my sweet little girl, and the next day, she had turned into a full-blown addict! Her eyes were sunken in, her body became a skeleton, and the color of her skin became a sickly shade of ashen gray and white. Then one day, I came home from working at the school and called out to Gloria. When she didn't answer me, I became nervous and looked around the house. There she was in the bathroom, and the sight was like that out of a horror scene. There she was, my poor baby girl, lying in the tub unconscious and just a few breaths away from death. The blood that dripped from her slit wrists had formed a large sticky pool on the tile floor. I will never forget that sight for as long as I live." Connie's eyes filled with tears. A ball formed in her throat, but she was determined to press on.

"The paramedics were able to save her from her attempted suicide, but that wasn't going to be the end for Gloria. She needed help, serious help. I enrolled her in a very good rehab, an expensive rehab, and picked up odd jobs here and there in order to pay for her treatment. It was still not enough to pay for her time there, so I dipped into my savings until it was all drained. I couldn't keep up with my mortgage payments and lost my house to foreclosure. I had to sell most of my furniture and household items and get a small apartment in order to keep a roof over my own head. Then as if things couldn't get any worse, Gloria had left the rehab, and I never heard from her again. I tried to get information as to where she might have gone, but they didn't know. I don't know if she went back to a life of drugs or what happened to her. She could be alive or dead today, and that is what hurts the most. My heart has been cracking a little more each day wondering where Gloria ended up."

Connie took an empty seat and sat down at the dining room table. All eyes were on her. The guests showed various expressions on their faces. Some showed sympathy, some showed astonishment, and some were so struck with awe as if they couldn't believe what was happening that all they could show was confusion. But the truth of the matter was that they were all witnesses to a confession of murder, a real murder.

Connie said, "Since she kept her mouth closed about the bullying, it took me a while to find out the real reason behind my daughter's tragic behavior. I had to ask various students, and some were not as forthcoming as others. Eventually, it became clear that the Boho Beauties had more influence than I had realized. But what could I have done back then? I couldn't press charges against them for bullying! If I tried that, I would be dismissed as an oversensitive mother who's trying to blame someone else for her own daughter's behavior. The police wouldn't think that it was the Boho Beauties' fault for Gloria's actions since school Beauties have always been a common factor in every generation. I had to simply hold my anger inside and continue to work. Each day, I prayed for my dear daughter to either return home or to at least let me know that she was okay.

"When I landed this job at the Serowik mansion, I was able to obtain a better life for myself. I lived inside the home, I had a large kitchen to cook and bake in, and the family truly appreciated me. I hope that you know, Margaret, that I felt I could stay here forever and be really happy." Connie looked meaningfully at Margaret, who, with tears in her eyes, nodded toward Connie. Connie returned her attention back toward Lieutenant Ram Nandyala.

"When Margaret had hired Joyce Galway as her event coordinator, I could not believe my luck! Not only was Joyce a Boho Bully, she was the leader of the clique. As soon as I saw her smug face, all the past anger that had seemed to diminish slowly throughout the years all came flooding back to my heart. I have learned to forgive over the years, but a mother never forgets the pain forced upon her baby. I had to make things right for Gloria, so I decided to plan very carefully my revenge. I approached Joyce and reminded her of who I was at the school. At first, she didn't know who I was but soon said, 'Oh yes! Ms. Dub! How nice it is to see you.' And that was that. We exchanged pleasantries, and she enjoyed sampling my baked goods. I pretended to help her plan out the food arrangements for the party, and then she brought in two of her friends saying that they were going to help her with the preparations as well as be actors at the murder mystery dinner. You could not even imagine for one moment what I was feeling when I saw that the other two women, Clara Morton and Gina Sorenson, were also members of the Boho Beauties. It was as if Satan had given them all to me as gifts, and all I had to do was to plan out the desirable vengeance I held inside for too long.

"I was ever so careful, yes, ever so careful so as not to give my true intentions away. Chatting with the girls, I found out where they liked to hang out. The night of Joyce's death, I had slipped a note in her purse before she left the Serowik home. Joyce never saw it coming. There she was, dressed to impress and waiting impatiently for me. When I approached her, she lifted her arms and asked what was so important that I should meet her outside Scootin' Boots. As I pretended to apologize, I quickly took out the knife, which had almost caused the death of my baby, and thrust it into her perfect flesh. The look on her face was epic. I still get a kick out of that look." Connie giggled to herself.

"Then over and over again, I stabbed the snob out of that woman, that woman who had done so much damage to so many people, not just Gloria—and it felt really good." Connie was breathing hard now. She was reliving that moment in its entirety and seemed to forget that she was in the dining room with a proverbial spotlight shining on her in front of a staring, wide-eyed audience.

"Clara's death was just as easy to do, but not as memorable, since she was only one of Joyce's followers and only did what Joyce told her to do," said Connie. "I made sure that I didn't slip a note to her. I realized that the note to Joyce was a bit risky. This time, I told Clara over the phone to meet me at the place she was planning to hang out, and that I needed to deliver something for her from the Serowik home. She agreed and told me to meet her at Crystal Chimes. It was literally that easy. Her guard was down, and we were safely hidden from any onlookers.

"Gina was also simple to kill. I just found out where she lived and made up some story about having a check for her from Mrs. Serowik for her services. That put her at ease, and she let me in. When her back was turned, I struck. Killing her was even simpler than the other two. I seemed to have lost all hesitation by then. I guess that's what happens when one practices a new skill." Connie smiled wirily.

"And now, Lieutenant, I realize that the game is up, and you have me caught."

"It seems so," said Ram. He looked up and nodded. Two of the servants standing alongside the wall stepped toward Connie and helped her out of her chair. One of them took a pair of handcuffs out of his jacket pocket and attached them to her wrists as he said, "Connie Wjoinowski, you are under arrest. You have the right to remain silent ..."

They led Connie out of the dining room and out the front door. The other servants looked toward Ram. He dismissed all the servants, who were actually police officers. The mime and Ms. Marple stood up.

"May we be excused as well, Lieutenant?" asked Ms Marple.

"Yes, Officer Reid and Officer Anderson. Thank you for your help this evening." The mime and Ms. Marple, two guests who were clearly not guests but police officers, nodded and left the room. Ram watched them go before turning to the remaining occupants.

"I do apologize for the elaborated method of revealing the murderer," Ram said. "It does seem an unusual way to go about things. However, I had a very good idea as to who the killer was, but I had little evidence against her. I figured that the only way to find out the absolute truth was to get her to confess." He spoke with solemn frankness. Clearly, solving this case did not make him feel as triumphant as others did.

The guests were all solemn. The atmosphere was like that at a funeral. Some of the guests lowered their heads. All eyes were filled with tears. Calista got up and left the room. She reappeared with a box of tissues. She walked around the table offering a tissue to each guest who gratefully accepted. The noise of noses blowing was the only sound heard. Sniffles rang out, and a loud sob erupted from Margaret, who was clearly not taking the events of this evening well. Richard placed a comforting hand on his wife's back and rubbed soothingly.

"Come on, Margaret," said Richard. "Let's get you to bed. You just need a good night's rest." He helped escort a pathetic-looking Margaret, sniffing and dabbing her eyes with her tissue, out of the room. Margaret then reappeared in the doorway of the dining room and said through sniffles, "Ladies and gentlemen, please resume the festivities, if there's anything left to be festive about." Then she turned to leave, and she and Richard ascended arm in arm up the stairs and out of sight.

Lieutenant Ram Nandyala and Sergeant Bartholomew Lee stood facing a crowd of guests whose jawbones had permanently fallen from their faces.

"Did. That. Really. Just. Happen?" asked Jason Thompson with disbelief in his voice.

"Yeah," said Connor Serowik softly, "that just happened."

"Are you okay?" asked Fitz to Calista. She nodded, but the expression on her face was not certain.

Ram spoke up, "Unfortunately, Sergeant Lee and I have to leave. If any of you have anything to add or have any questions, we'll be at the station during the next few hours. Good night." And with that, Lieutenant Ram Nandyala and Sergeant Bartholomew Lee made their final exit from the Serowik home.

Chapter 28

The following morning was just as somber as the final moments of the evening before. No one seemed to have much of an appetite for breakfast, so they settled for some coffee and some lightly buttered toast. Everyone was quiet while they ate, and soon the last of the guests were gone. Fitz had left earlier than the rest of the guests since he had to be at work by eight that morning. Erin and Jason left after breakfast with plans to spend the day together. Ingaborg seemed to have changed drastically since the night before, and her whole demeanor was now apologetic. Hans seemed more relaxed and happier to see this type of change in his wife. They could be seen holding hands when they exited the Serowik mansion.

A few months went by, and life had resumed itself in Temecula for the Serowik family. Calista and Fitz continued to see each other. She and Erin now had something in common to talk about at work, as far as the topic of romantic relationships, since Jason had asked Erin out, and they had been dating. Connor finally slowed his own pace down and enrolled in an online college, much to Margaret's delight. Cirenio Ulster resumed his job tending to the Serowik's landscape, and Christine would often be seen visiting him with a basket of food and drink to enjoy a picnic lunch together. Richard and Margaret had hired a new cook. She was not as good as Connie, but she was eager to please her new employers, and she was available during all hours of the day, so Margaret and Richard decided to give her a chance.

Chapter 29

At the Southern California Correctional Center for Women, Connie Wjoinowski, clad in her orange jumpsuit, sat on the bed in her cell. She was about to drift off to sleep when her cell gate slid open, and the guard called out to her. Connie had a visitor.

She walked with the guard into the room where visitors were allowed to talk to prisoners. Connie, who did not know of anyone who would bother to visit her, was curious as to whom the guard was referring to. The room was empty except for a young woman who sat alone at a little table. The woman was beautiful and had kind eyes. Her long, wavy chestnut hair cascaded down her back. Her makeup was simple and natural looking. The woman wore a tailored suit and looked official except for the kind demeanor she showed. All of a sudden, Connie stopped herself from walking closer to the woman. She couldn't believe it. Was that? Could it be?

"Gloria?" asked Connie meekly.

"Hi, Mom," answered the young woman, her eyes now brimming with tears. They ran up to each other and embraced. The guard cautioned them that they could only embrace once before the meeting and once to say goodbye, but that no touching was allowed in between the visit. Connie and the woman, whom she now knew to be her long-lost daughter, took a seat on either side of the table facing each other.

"I didn't know if you were alive or dead," Connie said. Her eyes were wet and swollen.

"I know, Mom. I'm sorry." Gloria's eyes were sad as she gazed at her mother.

"Oh no, Gloria. It's not your fault. If anything, it was my fault for not getting you the help you needed sooner."

"You couldn't have known, and I realize that now. Before I didn't, until a few years ago, and yeah, I did at first blame you for what happened to me. After the rehab, I left and went into a state-funded shelter for women. It was my way of keeping you from paying for any more treatment and for giving myself an escape from the whole mess I was in. I got to know some really good councilors there, and they helped me to sort out my problems and to place the appropriate blame on those truly responsible, myself included. Then I learned how to forgive those who had caused me harm, the Boho Beauties mostly, but also to forgive myself for letting their actions get to me and allow myself to be destroyed. My process of healing both physically and emotionally was gradual, but I was finally able to find my own strength and to use it to my advantage. I went to college and graduated with my psychology degree just this last June. There's a lot of girls out there who need help just like I did, and I intend to provide that help. I'm working at the same shelter that accepted me after rehab."

"I am so proud of you!" gushed Connie. She was crying now and had the biggest smile on her face. "Oh, Gloria!"

The two women stared across the table at each other, mother and daughter, catching up on the years lost and crying over regretful decisions.

"I'm sorry, Mom, that you're in here," said Gloria.

"I'm sorry too, Gloria. I'm sorry too."

Soon the guard called time, and the women stood. Before the two women embraced, they stared at each other, each one taking the other in and memorizing every physical feature that had almost been permanently faded. Then Connie embraced her baby one more time. She breathed in the scent of Gloria's hair and smiled with true contentment. Finally, they parted ways after a tearful goodbye and a promise to see each other again soon.

Chapter 30

Richard and Margaret Serowik, as well as their two children, were present at the party for Lieutenant Ram Nandyala. Tonight was his retirement party, and the entire police station was decorated from ceiling to floor with banners, streamers, balloons, and tons of food. Since the party was held at the station, no alcohol was served, but sparkling cider was served in champagne flutes. Fitz was there, and he and Calista clinked their glasses after a small toast between each other. Calista walked over to Lieutenant Ram Nandyala, who was standing next to Sergeant Bartholomew Lee, and gave him a warm hug. Bartholomew's girlfriend came up to Ram as well, hugged him, and offered her congratulations. Then she and Bartholomew walked off together to get a refill on their cider, leaving Ram and Calista alone.

"Why are you retiring now?" Calista asked Ram. "What I mean is, why retire now when you are still young?"

Ram nodded in comprehension. "Yes, well, you see, Calista, a very wealthy uncle of mine had died and had bequeathed everything he owned to me."

"Oh," said Calista, "I'm sorry about your uncle's death."

Ram answered, "Thank you, but he was old, and his death occurred over a year ago. I was just waiting to sum up a few of my cases, and when these recent stabbings happened and I was assigned to solve them, I just had to wait a bit longer until I could fully enjoy my inheritance."

"Gosh!" exclaimed Calista. "Well, Lieutenant, are you ready for a life of leisure?"

"Ah, Calista, it is now just Mr. Ram Nandyala from now on. No more of the title lieutenant for me. And yes, I am quite ready for a new life of leisure. I might travel a bit or maybe enroll in a yoga class. Whatever my future holds, it should be interesting."

Somehow, Calista figured that something else was lying in Ram Nandyala's future. She couldn't be certain, but she had this feeling that his ventures of solving crimes was not yet finished. One just didn't turn off his skills of detection, especially the excellent skills that Ram Nandyala possessed. She didn't voice these thoughts, however. She simply smiled and toasted to his retirement from the police force. Ram smiled back and drank down his sparkling cider.

All of a sudden, a voice rang out from the large crowd of celebrating guests, "It's time to cut the cake!"

About the Author

Tiffany Ryan Hayes is a free spirit who has travelled the roads of the United States in order to learn about various types of people and to experience the unique characteristics that each state provides. Tiffany has worked as a licensed Pharmacy Technician and has recently graduated with her Bachelor of Science degree in education. She also volunteers as a Disaster Service Worker, and helps to educate citizens on disaster preparedness. She resides in Temecula, California, with her husband and four children.

CPSIA information can be obtained
at www.ICGtesting.com
Printed in the USA
LVHW040158230719
624964LV00002B/504/P